"Hey, I'm not the enemy here," he protested with his hands up in surrender.

Deep color rose into her cheeks. "I'm sorry, Daniel. I know you're just trying to help, but as I've said before, I'm not leaving my home. I think I'm safe here, and besides, I have every confidence that you're going to catch this creep quickly."

"I can't do that without your help. What I need you to do is think back into your past. Not just the last month or so, but rather longer ago than that. Maybe a man you dated in the past or a girlfriend you had a falling-out with. Angelique, there's got to be something there and I can't do anything unless you give me some names."

Tears misted her eyes as she gazed at the note on the coffee table before them. A deep shudder went through her, making her look small and fragile.

Daniel reached out and drew her into his arms. She held herself stiffly against him, and he was about to withdraw his arms from around her when she melted into him.

MURDER IN DARK WATERS

CARLA CASSIDY

MIX
Paper | Supporting responsible forestry
FSC® C021394

To my daughter, Darlene,
who continues to bring light and love to my world.

Recycling programs for this product may not exist in your area.

ISBN-13: 978-1-335-69049-4

Murder in Dark Waters

Harlequin Enterprises ULC
22 Adelaide St. West, 41st Floor
Toronto, Ontario M5H 4E3, Canada
www.Harlequin.com

HarperCollins Publishers
Macken House, 39/40 Mayor Street Upper,
Dublin 1, D01 C9W8, Ireland
www.HarperCollins.com

Printed in Lithuania

Carla Cassidy is an award-winning, *New York Times* bestselling author who has written over 170 books, including 150 for Harlequin. She has won the Centennial Award from Romance Writers of America. Most recently she won the 2019 Write Touch Readers' Award for her Harlequin Intrigue title *Desperate Strangers*. Carla believes the only thing better than curling up with a good book is sitting down at the computer with a good story to write.

Books by Carla Cassidy

Harlequin Intrigue

A Bayou Investigation

Murder in Dark Waters

Marsh Mysteries

Stalked Through the Mist
Swamp Shadows
Hunted in the Reeds

Harlequin Romantic Suspense

The Scarecrow Murders

Killer in the Heartland
Guarding a Forbidden Love
The Cowboy Next Door
Stalker in the Storm

Visit the Author Profile page at Harlequin.com.

CAST OF CHARACTERS

***Angelique Santori*—**Her life is ripped apart when her mother, Mystique, is murdered, and now she finds her own life in jeopardy as she's targeted by an unknown assailant.

***Daniel LeCroix*—**Chief of police. He's determined not only to solve the murder that has occurred but also to protect the beautiful woman who has won his heart.

***George Trahan*—**He'd dated Angelique in the past. Has he developed an unhealthy obsession toward her?

***Charles Lathrop*—**He'd gone to Mystique in her capacity as a voodoo queen and wanted her to cast a love spell. He was angry when the spell didn't work. Did he kill Mystique, and does he now want to take revenge against Angelique?

***Marianne Lutgen*—**A party girl in the swamp. Is she angry that Angelique never hangs out with her? Angry enough to kill her?

Prologue

The full moon overhead cast down a pale silvery light, painting the swamp with ghostly fingers of illumination. Deep shadows danced amid the bushes and thicket that grew on either side of the narrow path.

Some people thought the swamp was a dark and mysterious place fraught with all kinds of danger, and it could be, but for Angelique Santori and her two sisters, it was home.

"I had so much fun tonight," Angelique's youngest sister, Monique, said.

"That's because Alex Whitmyer kept asking you to dance," Dominique, the middle sister replied. The three had spent the evening at the Voodoo Lounge, a popular dance bar in the small town of Dark Waters, Louisiana.

"Be careful with that one," Angelique said. Alex was a wealthy townie who had a terrible reputation for using women, especially young women from the swamp.

"Oh, you don't have to worry about me with Alex. I know he's a total creep, but he's very good-looking and is a great dancer," Monique replied.

In the faint shaft of moonlight, Dominique's wide smile was obvious. "So, basically you're just using Alex because he looks good on the dance floor."

Monique laughed. "That's it, and he makes me look good on the dance floor."

"Oh, what shallow women we are," Angelique said and they all laughed. There was nothing better than spending time laughing with her sisters.

By that time, they had arrived at Monique's small shanty. "Good night, ladies," she said. "I'll see you both sometime tomorrow."

Angelique and Dominique said their good-nights and watched as their sibling crossed the short bridge that would take her to her front door. Once she was safely inside, the two continued their walk toward Dominque's shanty.

"What do you have planned for tomorrow?" Dominique asked as they bent to go under the Spanish moss that hung like a lacy shroud from a bald cypress tree.

"Mama is going to take me around the swamp again and show me where she gets some of the medicinal plants she uses," Angelique replied.

"Ah, so another day of education for you," Dominique replied.

"Exactly. I swear, if I live to be a hundred years old, I still won't know everything Mama knows about the swamp," Angelique said. "What about you? Do you work tomorrow?"

"Yes, it's back to the grind serving the fine people of Dark Waters at the café."

They stopped walking as they reached Dominique's

shanty. “Are we getting together for dinner tomorrow night?” Angelique asked. “Last I heard Monique was going to fry up some fish for us all, but she didn’t mention anything about it.”

“As far as I know we’re still on for that. I think it’s set for six tomorrow evening, but if anything changes, I’ll give you a call. Good night, Angelique.”

“Sweet dreams,” Angelique replied.

She watched as her sister went across her bridge and into her place, and then Angelique continued on her way. Even though Angelique was the eldest of the three, at twenty-nine years old, she still lived at home with her mother.

More than anything, Angelique wanted to be a healer. She wanted to help people who were in emotional and physical pain, and there were many plants in the swamp that held medicinal properties. Nobody knew more about that than Angelique’s mother, Mystique Santori.

Right now, Angelique considered herself a student. Eventually she would strike out on her own, but for now, living with her mother worked for her and her mother appreciated the company. In fact, that’s a lot of what kept Angelique in her mother’s home. Her mother had a fear of living alone and liked having Angelique around.

Deeper and deeper she went into the swamp. The moonlight disappeared, unable to pierce through the thick foliage overhead. Still, she walked nimbly on the narrow paths, instinctively knowing where to step and where to jump to avoid pools of dark water.

She had grown up here and knew it like the back of her hand. Finally, the shanty came into view. It was high on stilts and even though it was after midnight, lantern light flowed from the windows.

Mystique was definitely a night person and often saw her clients in the middle of the night. The lights in the shanty indicated to Angelique that her mother was probably still awake.

She ran up the bridge, and when she reached the front door, she unlocked it and went inside. Unlike most of the shanties in the area, this one was relatively large, with a living area, the kitchen, a bathroom and three small bedrooms.

Inside, it smelled of green plants and summer flowers and the faint lavender and vanilla that were her mother's favorite scents. Angelique walked to her mother's bedroom door and knocked. "Mama, I'm home."

She paused and when no response came, she knocked again, this time a little harder. "Mama?"

Her mother was a light sleeper. It was unusual that she wouldn't answer Angelique. A bit of concern swept through Angelique. She twisted the doorknob and opened the door.

Mystique was in the bed, her hair a spill of rich darkness against the light pink pillowcase. She faced away from Angelique, who approached the side of the bed. "Mama?"

She reached out and lightly shook her mother's shoulder. The action caused Mystique to roll over to her back. For a moment Angelique couldn't make sense of what she saw.

Blood. Oh God, there was so much blood. It soaked the front of her mother's pink nightgown and it came from a gaping wound in Mystique's throat. Waves of shock kept Angelique rooted in place. Her mother's throat had been cut from ear to ear.

Finally, her inertia snapped and she stumbled back from the bed, releasing a scream of horror and of deep, overwhelming grief.

Chapter One

The funeral for Mystique Santori was not only well attended by most of the people from the swamp, but also by a huge crowd of people who lived in town as well.

Angelique sat between her sisters as Preacher Drew Perry extolled the many virtues of her mother. Even though his booming voice filled the large church, Angelique could hear snatches of whispers of several women behind her.

"…a powerful voodoo queen."

"…she used black magic," another woman said.

"I heard she could raise the dead."

Angelique knew the reputation her mother had. According to the people of Dark Waters, Mystique Santori had been a powerful woman, and it was said she got her power through black magic. Women and men came to her in the darkness of night, wanting a healing potion or a spell cast.

Angelique also knew her mother, and while Mystique could put on a good show for the clients who came to see her, she certainly had nothing to do with black magic or voodoo. She genuinely tried to help the people who came to her. More importantly, she had been a wonderful, loving mother and now she was gone…forever gone.

Tears burned at Angelique's eyes. It had been a week since she'd discovered her mother dead…murdered. During that week she had tried to stay strong for her sisters while they had cried a million tears.

Yesterday morning, Mystique had been cremated. There was no way she would have wanted to be on display in death. Each of the sisters had bought silver necklaces with a charm that held some of their mother's ashes.

Angelique had moved in with Dominique since the shanty had been declared a crime scene. But this morning, she'd been told she was free to go home tonight. Home…would it ever feel that way again without Mystique's loving presence?

Dominique squeezed her hand as Preacher Drew came to the end of his eulogy. The three sisters rose and walked down the long aisle to the church's front door.

The early June sun was hot overhead, and they continued down the walkway and then crossed the street to the community center. They had paid the café to cater food and for the next two hours friends would have a last chance to remember Mystique and tell her a final goodbye.

"I'm really dreading this," Monique said as they hit the sidewalk to cross the street.

"That makes two of us," Angelique admitted.

"It will be fine," Dominique replied. She was definitely the more social of the sisters. "Mama had friends who will need this closure."

They walked into the community center and Angelique looked around. The buffet was already set up on several long tables sporting white tablecloths. There was fried fish and baked chicken, macaroni and cheese and baked beans. There was also salad and fruit and slices of white cake for dessert. It was definitely a nice spread.

The rest of the room held four-top tables and chairs. They, too, were covered with white tablecloths. There was also a book on a pedestal for the guests to sign when they arrived.

The three stood by the front door as a small receiving line to the people who would come in. The first person through the door was Nola Fontenot, who had been a very close friend of Mystique's.

She hugged each of them as she cried. "I still can't believe this has happened," she said and pulled a tissue from her purse. "I'm going to miss her so much." She dabbed at her eyes. "If I can do anything for you all, just call me. Mystique would want you to come to me for anything you need."

Angelique hugged the plump older woman. "Thanks, Nola." Once Angelique released her, Nola signed the book and then moved on to sit at one of the nearby tables.

More people arrived, friends and acquaintances and the curious all greeted the sisters and then moved on inside. When the place was nearly full, the three of them sat at a table that had been reserved for them.

Angelique looked around, wondering if her mother's murderer was in the room. Tension twisted in her stomach. More than anything she wanted her mother's killer to be caught and sent straight to hell.

This thought had consumed her every waking hour since she had found her mother's body. Thank goodness her sisters hadn't seen their mother in death with her throat slashed open. That was a nightmarish image that would haunt Angelique for the rest of her life.

She was very unhappy with the lack of forward movement in the investigation into Mystique's murder, and so she had begun to do a little investigating of her own.

Over the past few days, she'd been interviewing the people she knew her mother was seeing in her official capacity as voodoo queen.

Chief of police Daniel LeCroix might be a handsome devil, but as far as Angelique was concerned, he was moving far too slowly in finding Mystique's killer. So far, he hadn't even checked in with her to let her know how the investigation was going.

Finally, things were winding down. Most of the people had left the community center, and a crew from the café was busy clearing the food tables.

"Whew, I'm glad this is all over," Monique said. Her long-lashed brown eyes misted with unshed tears. "But it won't really be over for us until we know who killed Mama."

"I'm determined to find the killer," Angelique said firmly.

"Be careful, Angelique," Dominique said with a

worried frown creasing her forehead. "The last thing we want is for you to get the attention of a murderer."

"Don't worry about me." She smiled with assurance at her two siblings. "I promise I'm not about to do anything stupid." As the eldest sister, Angelique had always known that her sisters looked to her for strength and guidance, and the last thing she wanted to do was worry or upset them.

The three were still seated at the table when Daniel LeCroix walked in the front door. With his dark, slightly shaggy hair, blue eyes and sculpted features, the chief was definitely a hunk. His blue uniform fit across his broad shoulders and his pants showed off his slim waist and hips.

On the night of the murder, when he and his men had responded to the scene, he'd been exceedingly kind to her and her sisters, but he didn't look so kind right now. His dark brows were pulled together and tension tightened his features as he approached where they sat.

His blue eyes looked directly at Angelique and he definitely looked angry. She raised her chin slightly and held his gaze. She had no idea why he might be angry with her, but she was definitely angry with him for the lack of progress and communication about the murder that had forever changed her life.

"Miss Santori," he said, once he reached where they were seated. "May I have a word with you…privately?"

Angelique rose from her chair. "Absolutely. There's a small patio out the back door. We can talk there."

He gave a curt nod of his head. "You can lead the way."

She had no idea what issue he might have with her, but she definitely intended to use this time to give him a piece of her mind.

DANIEL WALKED BEHIND the tall, dark-haired beauty, his anger with her rising with each step he took. They reached the back door and stepped out into the bright sunshine.

"What in the hell do you think you're doing?" he asked when she turned to face him.

Her cheeks flushed and her long-lashed unusual light brown eyes flashed with obvious irritation. "What are you talking about?" she asked.

"I'm talking about you trying to ruin my investigation." He couldn't help but notice how her long black hair sparkled like silk in the sunshine overhead.

"What investigation?" she asked with obvious derision. "You haven't checked in with us to tell us what's happening. Maybe because Mama was swamp, there is no urgency to solve the crime."

Daniel drew in several deep breaths. The woman was absolutely maddening. "That's definitely a low blow. Murder is murder, and I investigate it the same no matter where the victim comes from."

Her cheeks flushed with color and she averted her gaze from his. "You're right, that was a low blow." She looked at him once again.

Daniel raced a hand through his hair, a gesture of sheer frustration. "Look, you've got to stop questioning potential suspects. You meddling in this could completely ruin the prosecution of the killer when we find him."

"I… I hadn't thought of that." She raised her chin, a new blaze flashing in her gorgeous eyes. "But I've been so frustrated by the lack of communication from you. I don't know what you're doing to find her killer. I have no idea who you've questioned and who you haven't. I have no idea if you're actually working the case or sitting around and drinking coffee in your office."

Once again, an angry frustration filled Daniel. "Me and my officers have been out busting our butts on this case. But I need you to stay the hell out of it."

"Then tell me what you're doing, and I'll stay out of it," she replied. She frowned, the gesture doing nothing to detract from her loveliness. "Why don't you come by my place every night and tell me what you've accomplished during the day?"

"I could give you a check-in call each evening," he countered.

She shook her head. "That's not good enough. I need to see your face when you check in with me. Besides, coming by my place will show your utter commitment to the case. Promise me you'll do this and I'll promise to stay out of things."

It would be a total pain to do it, but at this point he would agree to almost anything to keep her from meddling in the case. Not only could she screw up the investigation, but she could also get hurt. The killer had already shown himself to be capable of committing a heinous crime.

"Okay, I can do that, but I can't promise what time I'll show up. It might be early in the afternoon or it might be late at night. It's possible there might be nights when I can't be there at all."

"I'll wait for you if it's late and if you can't show up in person, then call and let me know," she replied. She leaned forward and grabbed his forearm. Her touch instantly caused an unexpected spark of pleasure to go off deep inside him.

"Please, Chief LeCroix, I need to know what's happening. I'll never be able to get the image of my mother with her throat gaping open out of my head. The only thing that will help is knowing that you're doing everything you can to catch the person responsible." She dropped her hand from his arm as her eyes suddenly shimmered with tears.

Daniel's anger slowly seeped out of him, replaced by sympathy for her. She was as much a victim as her mother had been, and he understood her need for answers. Hell, he wanted answers, too.

He reached out and took her hand in his. "We're going to get the person who took your mother's life," he said. "I promise you, Miss Santori, we'll get this killer behind bars." He squeezed her hand and then released it.

"Please, make it Angelique," she said. "So, we have a deal. You'll come to my shanty and fill me in each evening and I'll stay out of things." She glanced toward the back door. "I need to get back inside. It's time we vacate the building."

Since they were in a courtyard, there was no way he could exit other than walking back inside with her, so together they went back into the building. Angelique's sisters both rose to their feet as Daniel headed for the front door.

He walked out into the bright sunshine, his head still filled with thoughts of the woman he had just left. Before the murder, he'd seen Angelique around town. He'd always thought she was one of the most beautiful women he'd ever seen.

He'd thought about asking her out, but at that time she'd been in a long-term relationship with Jason Webber, and after that he'd heard she was seeing George Trahan, a gator hunter and fisherman. Then the murder of her mother had occurred, and the last thing he needed to do was get involved with one of the victims in the case.

It was a short distance from the community center to the police station. As he walked, he looked up and down Main Street. A sense of pride filled him. The storefronts were all in colors of pink, turquoise and yellow, making the little town look colorful and full of life.

The police station was painted a bright yellow and as he walked through the front door, he smiled at Gus Smith, who sat at the receptionist's desk. Gus was very close to retirement age and had severe arthritis in his hips, so he was rarely out in the field. Instead, he spent most of his days on desk duty.

"Hey, Chief," Gus greeted him with a smile.

"What's up?" Daniel replied with a returning smile.

"Nothing much. It's been very quiet all morning. Not a single person has come in, and there haven't been any phone calls," Gus said. "I assume most of the folks were at the big funeral."

"Guess so," Daniel agreed. "And quiet is the way I like it. I'll just be back in my office." Daniel walked through the door to the left of Gus's desk and headed down the long hallway to his office.

Once there, he sat at his desk and checked for any messages that might have come in over the tip line that had been set up for Mystique's murder. So far, to his dismay, nothing had come in. There was a $5,000 reward for anyone who gave information on the murder that led to an arrest, but so far nobody had come forward with any information. The money had come from several businesses and both town and swamp people had contributed.

He'd only been in his office about five minutes when a knock sounded at his door. "Come in," he said and then grinned at the tall, dark-haired officer who entered.

"The ceremony was nice," Detective Clay Caldwell said. Clay was not only Daniel's right-hand man, but the two men had also been good friends since they were young kids.

"Yeah, and her killer was probably in attendance," Daniel replied with a frown. "Hopefully Luke wrote a list of everyone who was there." Detective Luke Madison was somebody else Daniel depended on both as a friend and as a coworker.

"He did. I think he also talked to Angelique about getting the guest book so we can make copies of the people who signed it."

"Good. After everything was finished, I had a little chat with Miss Angelique," Daniel continued.

Clay raised a dark brow. "How did that go?"

"Not well, although hopefully I made her see the error of her ways and I got her to agree to stay out of the investigation." He didn't mention how attractive he found the fiery woman or that she had demanded he give her nightly reports.

"I can't believe she interviewed Louis Theriot before we did," Clay said with a shake of his head.

"And who knows who else she spoke to in the past week," Daniel replied. "But hopefully that situation is now taken care of." He definitely hoped she'd keep her word and leave the investigation to him and his team.

"Good. What's on our agenda for this afternoon?" Clay asked.

"We need to speak to Nola Fontenot again. Hopefully, now that the shock of Mystique's murder has worn off, she can give us some more names of people Mystique was seeing or who might have had a beef with her."

"She wasn't very much help the first time we spoke to her," Clay reminded him. "I swear, I think she cried as much or more than Mystique's daughters did."

"Maybe she'll have less tears and more information for us this afternoon," Daniel replied. "According to the Santori sisters, she was Mystique's best friend. She should know something about Mystique that will help us find the murderer."

"I'll bet there are a lot of people in Dark Waters now quaking in their boots, wondering if they'll be outed for seeing the voodoo queen under the cover of the darkness of night," Clay said.

Daniel released a dry laugh. "If she was really a voodoo queen, then she wouldn't be dead right now, but I'm sure you're right about people worrying that their secrets will get out. Those are the very people we need to find. Whoever killed Mystique didn't rob her. The person didn't stand to gain anything financially from her death, so I'm betting that it was fear that killed Mystique. Somebody was afraid enough to slice her throat…possibly a symbolic act of making sure Mystique didn't talk."

"All I know for sure is her murder has really shaken some people up, both in town and in the swamp," Clay said, a frown furrowing his forehead. "And I have a feeling this isn't going to be an easy solve."

"I have a feeling you're right. One thing is certain, we aren't going to solve anything sitting around in here." Daniel rose from his chair. "Get Luke and the three of us will head into the swamp to speak to Nola again. We'll meet in about twenty minutes at the main entrance to the swamp."

"Got it." Clay got up and left the office, followed closely by Daniel.

Minutes later, Daniel was in his car and headed toward the swamp that half-surrounded the small town of Dark Waters. It had been well over a year since there had been a murder in town. At that time eighty-year-old Claude Breaux had shot his seventy-nine-year-old wife during a fight between the two. Apparently, she hadn't made his eggs right that morning and a verbal argument had ensued. In the end, Claude had grabbed his gun and shot his wife.

It had been an easy solve as Claude had come into the police department and crying uncontrollably, he'd confessed to the crime.

The murder of Mystique was a whole different animal. She had worked in the darkness of night and secrets had been her commodity. She had been a very powerful woman in the small town of Dark Waters, and powerful people made powerful enemies.

It had taken them two days to process her bedroom, seeking anything that might lead them to a killer. However, they had found nothing there to move the investigation forward.

His thoughts immediately shifted to Angelique. The three sisters were all pretty, but he found Angelique to be absolutely stunning. He tightened his hands on the steering wheel as he pulled to a stop in the small parking area in front of the swamp's entrance.

She was definitely beautiful, but he hadn't missed the defiance that had snapped in her eyes, or the stubborn rise of her chin as he had spoken to her.

He stared at the swamp ahead. The trail leading in was nothing more than a small path with thick vegetation on either side. It looked dark and mysterious but there were a lot of people who called the swamp home.

Mystique's shanty was deep in the swamp. Dark water surrounded it, along with tall tupelos and bald cypress trees. It was definitely going to be a pain to end his nights by going in to meet with Angelique.

However, she could either be a help or a hindrance in the investigation. While he understood her need to find her mother's killer, he would agree to almost anything to keep her out of his investigation.

Chapter Two

It was just after five that afternoon when Angelique carried her small suitcase from Dominque's place to her home in Mystique's shanty. Dread rose as a bitter taste in the back of her throat when she unlocked the front door and stepped inside.

She set the suitcase down and then stood for a long moment and stared at her mother's bedroom door. She needed to see the room and exorcise the memory of the last time she had seen her mother there. Her fingers trembled with emotion as she walked over and took hold of the doorknob.

She had no idea in what condition the police had left the room. With a deep breath, she opened the door. The mattress was now bare. Apparently, the police had taken the sheets and blanket with them as evidence when they had left.

It didn't smell like murder in here, rather the air still held the lingering soft lavender and vanilla scent of her mother. Grief squeezed Angelique's chest.

Considering the police had thoroughly searched the room, it was in surprisingly good shape. The only thing missing was Mystique. Once again Angelique's heart squeezed tight. She stepped back out of the room and closed the door behind her.

There was one other room she needed to check out. It was the smallest of the bedrooms and had been the room where her mother met her clients. The round table there was covered with a deep purple cloth and there were two chairs, one on either side.

A large scarf with images of the sun and moon and stars covered one of the walls, and there was a bookshelf next to where her mother would sit. The shelves held jars of salve, lotions and potions that she'd used, along with herbs and plants and other items.

This room had been searched as well. She could tell because some of the items were out of place. Again, she was pleased that at least the police hadn't trashed the room in an effort to search it for clues.

She went back to the front door, picked up her suitcase and then went into her bedroom. It was also a relatively small room, but she'd always found it cozy and comfortable.

There was a double bed, a dresser and two nightstands. The bed was covered in a lilac-colored spread and the single window held matching curtains. As she unpacked her things, her mind whirled in a million directions.

A renewed grief took hold of her and for several minutes she sat on the edge of her bed and wept. She'd tried so hard not to cry in front of her sisters, but now the suppressed tears from the past week fell.

She didn't know how long she wept before she finally managed to pull herself together. It was now close to six o'clock, and she had no idea what time Chief LeCroix might come by. And he'd better show up, she thought with a touch of anger.

She needed to know just how committed he was, to not only solving this crime but also keeping her up-to-date as to where the investigation was going. She had a right to know everything that was being done to find the killer.

However, she knew he was right that she shouldn't go running amok through his investigation, but over the past week she hadn't seen much of an investigation on his end happening.

Once her tears dried, she went out the back door to the deck that surrounded the shanty. She started up the generator that was usually run during her work and dinnertime.

She went back inside and plugged her phone in to charge and then pulled out a two-burner cooktop from under a kitchen cabinet.

She hadn't eaten much of the catered food earlier, and now a pang of hunger shot off in the pit of her stomach. There was no refrigerator, only a cooler packed with blocks of ice to keep things cold. Over the past week of her being gone, the ice had melted and the only thing that could be salvaged was a half a dozen eggs and some stale bread. Dinner was scrambled eggs and toast.

She cleaned up the mess and then moved into the living room, where she sank down on the sofa, her thoughts turning to Daniel LeCroix.

There was no question that he was one of the handsomest men she had ever seen. He had a reputation as a fair and just lawman. It had truly been a low blow for her to intimate that maybe he wasn't doing a thorough investigation because they were swamp people. From everything she'd heard, he was completely unbiased and treated both swamp and town people with the same level of respect.

She got back up and walked over to the bookcase that held dozens of books about swamps. She picked out one that she knew had been one of her mother's favorites and then settled back on the sofa to read.

It was one thing to read about plants in the swamp, but quite another to know where, exactly, in the swamp to find them. Among other things, she would miss her mother's teachings on such things.

She read for about an hour and then closed the book and began to pace the floor, her thoughts once again a tangled mess inside her head.

Who had killed her mother? And why? Why had this happened? Who could have wanted her dead, and in such a violent way? So many questions and no answers.

And when was Daniel going to arrive here to tell her what he'd accomplished that day to get her those answers?

It was almost nine o'clock when a knock fell on her door. She opened it and sighed with relief at the sight of him. She'd begun to think he wasn't going to show up at all, but he was here.

"Chief LeCroix," she said.

"Miss Santori." He nodded his head in a curt greeting.

"Please come in." She opened the door wider to allow him entry. As he swept past her, she caught the scent of his cologne. It was a fresh, woodsy scent with a hint of a citrus note. She immediately found it very attractive.

She gestured him to sit on the gray sofa while she sat in the matching chair across from him. Even though it was the end of the day, he still looked crisp and fresh in his uniform. She didn't offer him anything to drink. This wasn't a social call…this was strictly business.

"So, fill me in," she said as she leaned forward.

He raised a dark brow. "No *good evening* or *how are you doing*? No banalities at all?"

"I'm more of a get-to-the point kind of a gal," she replied.

"I'll keep that in mind in the future," he replied. He leaned back, and for the first time she noticed the tired lines at the outer corners of his beautiful blue eyes.

Despite that, his masculine presence seemed to fill the entire room. His energy radiated from him and it appeared that he commanded the space around him.

"I want to know what you did today, but I also want to know what you've done for the past week," she said. "Please," she added softly.

"As you know, it took several days for us to process the scene here. While my officers were doing that, I interviewed you and both your sisters. You all gave me a couple of names to follow up with, and so the next person I spoke to was Nola Fontenot, who you all indicated was one of Mystique's best friends."

"And what did you learn from her?" Angelique asked.

"Not a lot. She was quite distraught when we spoke to her and had very little to offer us at that time. After that, we interviewed Corrine Fortier, who Nola told us was a frequent visitor of your mother's. We also spoke to Helene Benoit, another client of your mother's."

"Do you really believe a woman killed her?" Angelique asked curiously. It was so hard to believe that a woman could have murdered her mother in such a heinous manner.

"At this point I don't know what to believe. Nola gave us some names of other women she knew who had dealings with your mother, but that was all we got out of her during our initial interview." He mentioned a few more women he'd spoken to over the past week. "Most of the people we talked to had solid alibis for the night of her murder."

"What was the time of the murder?" Had it occurred only minutes before Angelique had gotten home? If she'd come home earlier, would she have been able to stop the murder from happening. She hadn't heard from anyone what the exact time of her mother's death had been.

"The coroner fixed her time of death at around ten o'clock," he replied.

"If only we hadn't gone out that night," Angelique said as a new burst of grief tightly squeezed her heart. "If only I'd stayed home."

"Don't do that to yourself, Angelique." His voice was deep and soft. "Don't take on any blame for what happened. There's only one person to blame in this, and that's the killer. I swear we're going to find that person, Angelique."

"You promise?" Tears misted her vision, but she swallowed hard against them so they wouldn't fall. The last thing she wanted to do was cry in front of Daniel LeCroix.

"I promise," he replied, a steely determination in his voice that comforted her. "This afternoon we spoke with Nola once again, and she had a couple more names for us."

"Like who?" she asked.

"Charles Lathrop. She remembered your mother talking about him. Apparently, he came to her for a love spell."

"Is it possible the spell didn't work and so he was angry? Angry enough to kill her…to slash her throat?" she asked.

"That's what we need to find out. We tried to chase him down today, but yesterday he left town on business. He's supposed to be back on Friday. So, we'll catch up with him sometime tomorrow."

"I was usually in my room when I knew somebody was coming to speak to Mama. Most of the time I didn't know who she was seeing." She frowned. "I should have paid more attention to who was coming and going from here."

"There you go, blaming yourself again," he chided.

She smiled at him and when he returned the gesture, a spark of attraction shot off inside her. The man had an amazing smile that revealed his straight, white teeth and lit up all his features. "So, what other names did Nola come up with?" she asked.

"Oliver LeBeouf, Lucinda Reese and Pierre Guidry. We interviewed Oliver and Lucinda, but when we went to Pierre Guidry's shanty to speak to him, he wasn't there. So, we plan to catch up with him in the morning."

"There might be some bad blood there," Angelique said. "He was my mother's lover off and on for years, and when she stopped seeing him about two months ago, he was very angry. But he loved her desperately, and I can't imagine him ever hurting her, let alone killing her."

"What about George Trahan?"

She looked at him in surprise. "George? Why would he have an issue with my mother?"

"Nola told me Mystique didn't like the guy very much and that might be the reason you stopped seeing George," he replied.

A small laugh escaped her. "I stopped seeing George because I knew the relationship wasn't going to go anywhere. He's a nice man, but I didn't have any real romantic feelings for him. Besides, I hear he's quite happy with Desiree Augustin now."

"Anyway, that's what we accomplished today and we have those several people to interview tomorrow."

"So, there are no real suspects right now," she replied.

"You're lucky that so many people saw you at the Voodoo Lounge at the time of your mother's murder, otherwise you would have been my top suspect."

"You investigated me?" she asked in stunned surprise.

"You and your sisters were the first people I investigated," he replied. "Think about it. You, more than anyone else, would have had the opportunity. But of course, I know you didn't do it, and right now, nobody has risen to the top of a suspect list. There was no forced entry, so she either let her killer inside or the killer had a key. Do you have any idea who might have keys?"

She shook her head. "I would have no idea. Nola might have had a key, and it's very possible Pierre had a key, but I would assume Mama got it back when she broke things off with him."

He leaned forward. "Angelique, all we can do is follow the leads we get. Much of what your mother did was in secret, which makes our job even harder."

"I know she kept a book of her clients, but I haven't seen that book since her murder," Angelique replied as she realized she should have told him sooner about the tome.

"What did the book look like?" he asked, a new urgency in his voice.

"It was a blue hardback notebook with the moon and stars on the cover. I really haven't had a chance to look for it. To be honest, I just now thought about it. But tomorrow I'll check out her room and see if it's there somewhere."

She frowned at the thought of going back into Mystique's room, where that soft lavender scent of her mother still lingered in the air.

"A book like that would definitely be helpful in the investigation," he replied.

She nodded. "Hopefully I can find it tomorrow, and when I do, I'll call and let you know I have it. I'm sorry I didn't think about it sooner. To be honest, I haven't been thinking very clearly since her murder."

"I understand how difficult this time has been for you and your sisters," he replied. There was a softness in his gaze, and for just a moment she wanted to fall into the blue depths.

What would it feel like for his big strong arms to embrace her? Would that give her back her sense of security? Would that make her grief lessen? She mentally shook herself. What was she thinking? All she wanted from Daniel LeCroix was answers to her mother's murder.

"You do realize my mother often met her clients at their homes as well as meeting them here," she said.

He nodded. "We know that, but whoever killed her came here. Anyway, that's where we are right now." He stood and she did as well. "I can promise you I haven't been sitting in my office and drinking coffee all week."

She felt the heat of a blush dance into her cheeks. "I was very frustrated when I said that, and I do apologize."

"Apology accepted," he replied with a humorous glint in his eyes. He walked toward the door and she trailed behind him. She couldn't help but notice that the man looked as good going as he did coming. He stopped at the door and opened it and then turned back to look at her.

"Then I'll see you tomorrow night?" she asked.

"That's our arrangement," he agreed.

"Thank you for this," she replied. The scent of his cologne threatened to half dizzy her senses. "I just… just really need to be involved in the hunt for my mother's killer."

"Okay, then you sit and drink coffee all day and I'll keep you involved in the case each evening. Goodnight, Angelique."

"Good night, Chief LeCroix." She watched as he disappeared into the darkness, and then she closed the door and locked it for the night.

She sank down on the sofa and thought about everything he'd told her, but her thoughts lingered on Daniel the man and not on Daniel the lawman.

He was not only hunky looking, but she liked the way he smelled, too. It was obvious he had a good sense of humor, and she also found that very attractive. She also knew he was an available bachelor.

At the age of twenty-nine, Angelique had dated a lot of men, but somehow or another they always disappointed her in the end.

She had believed herself madly in love once before. Jason Webber was an insurance agent in town, and the two had dated for a little over a year. Angelique had believed they were both on the same page and eventually they would marry and build a family together. They had talked about those plans and she'd expected him to propose. But that hadn't happened.

Unfortunately, Jason had been a cheater and a liar, and he'd had no real interest in marrying Angelique. With all his lies and infidelity, he'd broken her heart into a million pieces.

That had been a little over a year ago. George Trahan had been the last man she'd dated. He'd been an experiment of sorts to see if there was a chance for her to experience love once again, even though Jason had left her with a general distrust of all men.

After seeing George a couple of times and knowing he was developing feelings for her that she didn't share, she'd stopped seeing him. Now she was no longer interested in dating. She didn't believe real love existed. She had decided she would live alone and take lovers when she wanted like her mother had done.

She definitely had no interest in any kind of personal relationship with the chief of police, no matter how attractive she found him. All she wanted from him was answers as to who had killed her mother. And why.

DANIEL SAT AT his desk early the next morning, thinking about his interaction with Angelique the night before. She'd smelled of summer flowers and mysterious spices, a scent he found very attractive.

She had looked beautiful in a pair of jeans that had hugged her long legs and a pink sleeveless blouse that had showcased her slender waist and her full breasts. There was no question that she was a stunning woman, but she would probably be a hellcat to live with.

The last thing Daniel wanted was to hook up with a

controlling woman. Been there, done that. His seven-month-long relationship with Allison Gregory had left such a bad taste in his mouth he hadn't dated for the past year.

Allison had been beautiful, too. They had dated for three months, and then she had moved in with him. Suddenly she was trying to control everything in his life, and if he didn't allow her to do so, she threw a hellish temper tantrum or would pout for days on end.

No, there was no way in hell he would have a relationship with Angelique Santori. He grabbed his coffee cup, took a drink and then mentally shook himself.

What was he doing sitting here and even thinking about Angelique Santori? All she wanted from him was answers and nothing more. And he hoped he could give them to her sooner rather than later.

It might have been easier if he'd known about the book Mystique kept earlier. If she had chronicled the names of her clients, then it was possible the murderer's name could be listed there. He'd love to get his hands on that book.

He'd checked the list of items taken into custody following the murder, but there was no book listed. Hopefully Angelique would find it today and turn it over to them. It could be the very key to solving the murder.

The bloodstained sheets and blanket from Mystique's room had been sent to a lab to see if it was possible the killer's blood was also there. But it would probably take weeks before they got the results.

It was just past eight when Daniel, Clay and Luke left the police station. First, they were headed to

George Trahan's shanty to interview him. Was it possible the man had killed Mystique because she hadn't approved of him as a suitor for Angelique?

It was a long shot, but Daniel didn't intend to leave any stone unturned going forward, so they would speak to George and see if he had an alibi for the night of Mystique's murder.

The three of them rode in Daniel's car and as he drove, he told them about the book. "That book could crack this case wide-open," Luke said from the passenger seat.

"Are we sure one of Mystique's clients murdered her?" Clay asked. He was seated in the back, behind Daniel.

"No, at this point we aren't sure of anything," Daniel replied. "However, that book would definitely help us. Angelique is going to check around the house to see if she can find it."

"Now that is one strong woman," Clay said.

"I definitely wouldn't want to get on her bad side," Luke added. "I have a feeling she could chew a man up and spit him out with no problem."

"She just wants her mother's murder solved," Daniel said, surprised to find himself wanting to defend her. Heck, at this point he didn't even know if he liked the woman, not that it mattered.

By that time, he had pulled to a halt at the swamp's entrance and they all got out of the car. "Do you know where George's shanty is located?" Clay asked.

"I have a general idea," Daniel replied. Over the

past week of the investigation, he had become more familiar with who lived where in the swamp.

The swamp was a close-knit community where everyone seemed to know everyone's business. Daniel was hoping to connect with somebody who knew something about the murder of one of their own.

He followed the narrow trail into the dense vegetation. Small animals scurried out of his way and overhead birds squawked from the treetops. Fish jumped in a large pool of water they passed on the right.

They walked by several shanties and finally came to the one where George Trahan resided. George was a gator hunter and fisherman. The shanty was relatively small, and when Daniel knocked, the door was opened by Desiree Augustin.

Desiree was tall and lean and quite attractive. Her dark eyes widened at the sight of them. "Chief LeCroix," she greeted.

"Hi, Desiree. We need to speak with George. Is he here?" Daniel asked.

"Yeah, he's in the kitchen. Come on in." She opened the door wider to allow them entry.

They entered into a small living room with a cot shoved against one wall, obviously acting as a sofa, and a wooden rocking chair. The space was neat and clean, and as Desiree gestured them to sit on the cot, George entered the room.

George greeted them all and then sat in the rocking chair facing them, his dark brows raised in obvious curiosity. Desiree stood by his side, a hand on his shoulder.

George was a big man, with broad shoulders and a thick chest. Unlike most of the gator hunters who wore their hair long, George's dark hair was short and neatly trimmed. However, his brows were heavy, giving him a slightly menacing look even when he smiled. So, this was the man Angelique had dated, Daniel thought.

"Gentlemen, what can I do for you this morning?" he asked in obvious curiosity.

"We'd like to ask you a few questions," Daniel said. "Perhaps there's someplace we could go to speak to you in private?"

"This is fine. I don't have any secrets from Desiree." He smiled up at the woman, and she patted his shoulder with a smile of her own.

"I understand you were dating Angelique Santori for a while," Daniel said.

"I was," George replied. "She's a beautiful woman. She's very bright, and it was a real pleasure to spend time with her. I dated her for about a month before she broke things off with me."

"I also understand that Mystique wasn't a big fan of yours," Daniel continued.

George laughed. "Yeah, she made it very clear from the get-go that she didn't think I was good enough for her daughter."

"Did that make you angry?" Daniel asked.

"Not angry enough to kill her," George replied, his dark eyes slightly narrowed. "I had nothing to do with Mystique's death. I had absolutely no reason to kill her."

"Maybe you believed that she got Angelique not to see you anymore," Daniel replied.

George laughed once again. "Have you met Angelique Santori? Nobody tells that woman what to do."

"Where were you on the night Mystique was killed?" Luke asked.

"I was right here with Desiree," George replied without hesitation.

"I can tell you he was here with me all night," Desiree said.

"I'm telling you I had absolutely no reason to kill Mystique," George said. "I've moved on. I started seeing Desiree again, and I'm very happy in my relationship with her."

"Do you know who might have wanted her dead?" Daniel asked.

George shook his head. "I'm sorry, but I don't have a clue."

"So, what do you think?" Luke asked a few minutes later as they left George's shanty.

"I don't think he's our man," Daniel replied. "He's right in that he had no reason to kill Mystique. We'll head on to Pierre Guidry's place and see what he has to tell us."

"He's the guy who had a personal relationship with Mystique?" Luke asked as they headed deeper into the swamp.

"According to Angelique, he was Mystique's lover for years. Nola told me there was some bad blood between them at the time of Mystique's murder."

"So, he's a very likely suspect," Clay said.

"We'll soon see." Daniel continued to lead the other two men along the narrow trail. It was a hot and sunny day, but they were now deep enough in the vegetation that it was a bit cooler and the sun couldn't quite pierce through the leaves overhead.

When he'd come out here the day before, he'd had to ask several people for directions to Pierre's shanty. He knew very little about the man other than, like George, he was a gator hunter. He was hoping this early in the morning, the man would be in his shanty and not out somewhere in the swamp.

He came to a fork in the path and took the narrower one that veered off. Once again animals rustled the brush on other side of them, and there were pools of water they had to either jump over or maneuver around.

Finally, they reached Pierre's shanty. It was a small, badly weathered structure with a porch that listed slightly to the right. Daniel knocked on the door. There was no reply. He knocked once again.

"All right, all right," a deep voice yelled from within. After a couple of moments, the door flew inward and Pierre glared at them all. He was a tall, muscular guy with long black hair that hung on either side of his strongly sculptured facial features. Daniel guessed the man to be in his mid-to-late sixties, but physically he was in great shape.

"What in the hell is going on here?" He was clad in a gray T-shirt and a worn pair of jeans that had holes in the knees. "What are you all here for?"

"Pierre, we have some questions for you. Can we come in?" Daniel asked.

Pierre hesitated a moment. "It's not exactly company ready in here," he said as he then opened the door to allow them in.

The interior of the shanty was as dismal as the outside. It was one room with a potbellied stove in one corner and a cot covered in a gray sheet shoved against another wall. Several articles of clothing hung from a makeshift closet and the kitchen consisted of two cabinets and a small countertop.

It smelled gamy, the odor mostly emanating from a shelving unit that held large rusty hooks, thick fishing line and various kinds of bait to catch gators.

"As you can see, this place isn't built for entertaining," Pierre said. "So, let's make this fast. I'm assuming you're here about Mystique's murder. That woman was my soulmate. I loved her with all my heart and soul. We loved passionately and we fought just as passionately."

"A crime of passion, people could understand that," Daniel said softly. "Is that what happened, Pierre? Maybe you went to talk to Mystique about getting back together with her and the two of you fought and somehow things got out of control?"

Pierre took a step closer to Daniel, his features twisted with anger. "Didn't you hear me the first time? I loved that woman and could never hurt her like that." The man's eyes appeared to darken and his hands fisted at his sides. "I didn't kill her, although I'd sure as hell like to know who did."

"That's what we're trying to find out," Daniel replied. "Where were you on the night she was murdered?"

"I was out in the swamp…hunting a particular gator I want to catch." Pierre's nose thinned as he drew in a deep breath and then released it. "I was alone and I was out most of the night."

"Did anyone see you out and about that night?"

"I doubt it," Pierre replied.

"Do you know of anyone else who might have wanted to harm Mystique?" Daniel asked.

"No, not off the top of my head. So, are we done here?"

"If you think of anyone let me know. Pierre, don't go off half-cocked on your own. I wouldn't want to have to lock you up."

"Got it," he replied tersely.

"I'm serious, Pierre," Daniel said.

"I said I got it," Pierre said. "Now, are we done?"

"RIGHT NOW, I'd say he's our number one suspect," Daniel said, once the men were on their way back to their car.

"He's got no alibi for the night of the murder," Luke said.

"And I would say the man definitely has a temper," Clay added.

"It's very possible he went to Mystique's that night in order to get their relationship back on track," Daniel said.

"Maybe this time Mystique was through with him

for good and when she told him that, he flew into a wild rage and he wound up slashing her throat," Luke said.

"All we have to do is prove it," Daniel replied.

On the way back to the station they drove through The Burger Joint, a drive-through that served a variety of fast-food sandwiches. They carried their lunches back to a small conference room that had been dedicated to the solving of Mystique's murder.

On top of the table were photos from the crime scene, along with reports from the interviews that had taken place so far. There were also a few notes on the large whiteboard that kept track of the investigation. Unfortunately, it was pretty bare at the moment.

They cleared spaces on the table and then sat to eat their lunch. As they ate, they talked about what they'd done so far and what they intended to do next.

Once they were finished eating, Daniel wrote George Trahan and Pierre Guidry on the whiteboard. He put a star next to Pierre's name. They had their first official suspect.

"Let's head out to Charles Lathrop's house and have a chat with him about the love spell Mystique did for him," Daniel said. "According to his personal assistant, he was supposed to be back in town by ten this morning."

He wasn't sure where the investigation would go next, as they had interviewed everyone Nola had told them about and those who they knew had visited Mystique as clients.

What would really help was getting his hands on the book that Mystique had kept on her clients. However, he hadn't heard anything from Angelique to let him know she'd found it.

He was surprised to realize he was looking forward to touching base this evening with Angelique. He only wished he was bringing her what she wanted most—the name of her mother's murderer.

Chapter Three

It was just before seven that evening when Daniel crossed the bridge to Angelique's front door. He knocked and she answered almost immediately.

Again tonight she was clad in a pair of jeans and a sleeveless bright red blouse that emphasized her dark beauty. Her long, dark hair was pulled back and tied at the nape of her neck with a red ribbon. She smiled as she greeted him and again that crazy tiny spark ignited in the pit of his stomach. God, she had a beautiful smile.

"Come on in," she said and opened her door to allow him entry. "Please, have a seat. Would you like a cup of coffee? I just made a pot."

"Last night I had the distinct feeling you probably wouldn't have offered me a cup of water if I was on fire," he said in open amusement. "But if you're offering, I'd love a cup of coffee."

"Normally I'm not so inhospitable as I was last night," she replied. "How do you like your coffee?"

"Black is just fine." He eased down on the sofa

while she disappeared into the kitchen area. As he waited, he looked around the room.

It was a nice space with a pot-bellied stove in one corner, the gray furniture and a large gray-and-yellow braided rug that nearly covered the floor. Green plants and a bookcase filled with books and battery-operated lanterns that cast soft illumination added to the cozy feel of the place.

This room was a far cry from the bedroom where Mystique met her clients. That small bedroom had felt otherworldly with its mysterious potions and lotions and the dark purple and deep blue wall hangings.

Mystique's bedroom had been a typical woman's bedroom with a pink bedspread and matching curtain at the window. There had been shelves in there as well, some filled with books and others full of body lotion, perfumes and jewelry.

Angelique came back into the room, carrying the two cups of coffee. He rose to take one from her, and she set the other one on the coffee table and then sat on the opposite end of the sofa from him.

Instantly he could smell the scent of her, that floral, slightly spicy fragrance he found so attractive. "How are you this evening, Chief LeCroix?" she asked with a hint of a smile.

So, the lady did have a sense of humor after all. "I'm doing okay…and you?"

"I'm hanging in there," she replied. "Is that enough banality for now?"

"It will do," he replied. He took a sip of the coffee and then set the cup down. "Today we touched base with George Trahan, Pierre Guidry, Charles Lathrop and Marie Witherspoon."

"I forgot all about Marie," she said, and a tiny frown danced into the center of her forehead, in no way detracting from her loveliness. "I would never believe that Marie had anything to do with my mother's death. She's a timid woman who was seeing my mother for self-confidence charms and spells."

"It didn't take us long to know she had nothing to do with this. In fact, she had a solid alibi. At the time of your mother's murder, her and her husband were having drinks at Frankie's," he replied.

Frankie's was a small bar where the older people in town usually went for drinks and quiet conversation. It was a much different experience from the Voodoo Lounge, where the music was loud and the crowd was young.

"I also know George had nothing to do with this. He had absolutely nothing to gain from my mother's death. We were not seeing each other at the time of the murder, and he was already seeing Desiree," she said. "He wasn't angry with my mother so I believe he's completely innocent."

She lifted her cup and took a drink and then cradled it in her hands, as if needing the warmth it could provide her. Maybe talking about her mother's murder filled her with a chill. If so, a new wave of sympathy for her worked through him.

"Then we have Charles and Pierre," he continued. "We met with Charles this afternoon, and he confessed to us that he was quite angry at your mother because the love spell she did for him didn't seem to be working, but he insisted he had nothing to do with her murder."

Her honey-colored eyes held his in an intense gaze. Lordy but her eyes were gorgeous with long, dark lashes. "Did you believe him?"

"He's on my potential suspect list. He couldn't provide a good alibi. He said he was home alone on the night of the murder. By the way, just for my own curiosity how does a love spell work?"

A quick smile lifted the corners of her lush lips. "The love spells my mother did certainly didn't involve any magic or voodoo, although she had a whole routine she did. She took a lock of hair from the client and then had them write the name of the person they wanted to charm on a small piece of paper. She wrapped the paper and the hair in a silk cloth. She then said some mumbo jumbo over it and then told him to bury it in his yard."

Her eyes appeared to darken with pain. She took a drink of her coffee and then continued. "You have to understand that the real power of a love spell is to give that person the self-confidence to make a move or whatever on the person they want. That's what it's all about. Sometimes it works and sometimes it doesn't, but in the end, it's really all up to the client."

"Interesting," he replied. So, it was all about empowering the client to act on his love interest. "Anyway, that now brings us to Pierre."

He paused as she took another drink of her coffee and then set the cup down on the coffee table. She leaned forward slightly. "What did you find out from him?" she asked.

"I would guess that your mother's relationship with him was quite tumultuous."

"You would guess right. They fought and made up dozens of times. My mother was a very headstrong woman, and Pierre is a very stubborn man. But I believe he loved my mother very much."

"He told us that she was his soulmate, and right now he's also my number one suspect."

"Really?" Her eyes widened in surprise. "So, you believe he killed my mother?"

"It's easy to speculate that Pierre came here that night to try to make up with your mother. Things didn't go his way and your mother told him she didn't want to get back with him. They fought and things got out of control and in a heat of passion, he slit her throat."

"But that's just speculation," she said.

"Correct. But given their personal relationship and the fact that Pierre has no solid alibi for that night puts him at the top of my list of suspects," he replied.

"How many people are on your list of suspects?" she asked.

It was his turn to take a drink of his coffee. He set the cup back down. "Two. Right now it's Pierre and Charles, but we're still investigating. By the way, did you find that book?"

She frowned once again. "No, and I looked everywhere Mama would have kept it. I think maybe it was stolen on the night of the murder."

He frowned as well. "That adds a whole new layer

to the investigation. Who would want that book badly enough to kill for it?"

"I have no idea, but it had to be somebody who knew about the book's existence, and I'm sure my mother didn't tell too many people about it." Tears suddenly shimmered in her lovely eyes. "I would have gladly given that book to somebody in order to save my mother's life."

The tears spilled over onto her cheeks. She swiped at them but they kept on falling. Daniel couldn't stand it. He had never liked to see a woman cry.

He stood and held out a hand to her. She looked up at him and then slid her hand into his. He pulled her up and into his arms as she began to cry in earnest.

She held herself stiffly against him for a long moment, and then she raised her arms, encircled his neck and melted against him.

As she sobbed into the crook of his neck, he caressed her slender back in an effort to comfort her. Despite the circumstances, he couldn't help but notice that she fit perfectly against him.

Her hair smelled clean and with the faint scent of strawberries, and then there was that floral, spicy scent that emanated from her. She definitely smelled good.

She cried for only a couple of minutes and then stepped back from him. "I'm sorry," she said as she quickly swiped at her cheeks, obviously embarrassed. "I am so sorry. I didn't mean to cry."

"Please don't apologize," he replied. "You obviously needed a good cry."

She took another step back from him as she wiped

the last of the tears from her face. "I've tried to be so strong, especially for my sisters. They need me to be strong."

"But, sometimes you just need to allow yourself time to grieve and to cry," he replied softly.

"I know. I just didn't expect to cry now," she said.

"It's okay. Well, I've caught you up on everything we've done, so I'll just get out of here now," he said.

She nodded and walked with him to the front door. When he reached the door, he turned back to look at her once again. "Are you sure you're all right?" he asked.

For the first time since he'd known her, she looked small and fragile. "I will be," she replied. "I'll see you tomorrow night?"

"Of course," he confirmed. "Good night, Angelique."

"Good night, Daniel," she replied.

He stepped out into the darkness of the night as she closed the door behind him. He turned on his flashlight to help guide him out of the dark swamp as his brain whirled with a million thoughts and impressions.

Angelique Santori. She'd definitely surprised him tonight with her soft vulnerability, and it made him wonder how many other facets there were to the woman. Not that it mattered. Not that he was really interested in her. Although he could admit he was definitely intensely physically attracted to her.

By the time he returned to his car, his thoughts had turned back to the case. The missing book was a new kink in the investigation.

Had Mystique put the book someplace where nobody would find it, or had it been stolen on the night of the murder? And if it had been stolen, had it simply been a case of opportunity after the murder had occurred, or had somebody specifically killed Mystique to get the book?

He had a feeling he'd be seeing a lot of Angelique, because this case wasn't going to be solved easily.

AFTER DANIEL LEFT, Angelique sank back down on the sofa and continued the cry she'd stopped short. She'd been so embarrassed to shed the tears in front of Daniel. However, she would admit that it had felt good to be held in his big, strong arms. It had felt very good to just give in and melt against his body as she'd wept.

She only cried for a little while longer, and then she got up and took the coffee cups into the kitchen. She washed them with the bottle of water she kept for that purpose and then put them back into the cabinet. Once that was done, she dumped the last of the coffee and washed the pot. Finally, she went out the back door and turned off her generator.

For several long moments she stood at the deck's railing. The moon was bright overhead and reflected beautifully on the dark waters below.

The thought that her mother had been murdered for the book where she kept her client's names and why they were seeing her mother not only devasted her, but also confused her.

Why on earth would anyone want such a book? And want it badly enough to kill for it? Or did the book have nothing to do with the murder? Had Angelique just not found the book yet and it was tucked away someplace in the shanty? So many questions and so far, there were no answers to any of them.

She looked around the area and a chill suddenly walked up her spine. She had the distinct feeling that somebody was watching her. This wasn't the first time in the past week that she'd felt this way.

She turned and went back into the shanty, locking the door after her. She assumed the crazy, paranoid feeling was simply a by-product of the murder.

Even though it was still relatively early, she got ready for bed. Once she was in her nightgown, she went around and turned off all the lanterns and carried one of them with her into her bedroom.

She placed the lantern on her nightstand and then turned it off. She slid into the sheets and the last thought she had was of how nice it had felt to be held in Daniel's arms.

She awakened early the next morning. She started the generator and then grabbed a towel and her bath gel and went out onto the back deck to take a shower. The shower was basically a wooden box with a large bottle of rainwater that was hooked to a hose and a spray nozzle.

The water was nice and warm from the sun. She washed with the shower gel and then shampooed her hair with a bottle that she kept in the bottom of the shower.

There was no time to linger as the water supply was very limited. Once she was finished, she dressed in a pair of jeans and a short-sleeved turquoise blouse.

Today was Dominique's day off from the café, so the three sisters were meeting to have breakfast together.

Angelique made her money by medical transcription and making phone calls urging patients to pay their bills for several of the doctors in town. It was something she could do from the comfort of home and the pay was terrific.

She was saving her money to eventually open a store in town that would sell the lotions and salves her mother had made for a variety of ailments among other things.

She almost had the money she needed and was excited at the prospect of being a shopkeeper. It had been her dream for a long time and she was getting so close to realizing it.

At nine fifteen she left the shanty and headed out. Her car was parked outside the swamp's entrance in a spot where other cars were parked that belonged to the people in the swamp.

Dominique was already there waiting for her, looking beautiful in a pair of jeans and a bright red blouse. Her long hair was pulled back at the nape of her neck and tied with a red ribbon.

"Hey, sis." She greeted Angelique with a wide smile. "Are you ready for breakfast?"

"I am, in fact I'm starving this morning." She gave Dominique a quick hug. "How are you doing?"

Dominique's smile faltered. "I'm doing okay. To be honest, I still can't believe she's gone."

"I know, but I also know that Daniel… I mean Chief

LeCroix is working hard to solve the crime and find the killer for us."

Dominique raised a dark brow. "Daniel?"

"That was just a little slip of the tongue," Angelique replied with a small laugh. "I'm getting nightly reports from him on where the investigation is going. But enough about that, we're going to go and enjoy our breakfast together."

"If Monique ever gets here. I swear that girl is always late," Dominique said.

"Hey, I heard that," Monique said as she stepped out of the green vegetation and approached where the other two stood.

Within minutes, the three of them were in Angelique's car and headed into town. She tried to keep the conversation light while she drove and thankfully her sisters followed her lead.

They had all grieved long and hard in the days following the murder, but life moved on and now it was time to move forward in the best way they possibly could. That's what their mother would have wanted for the three of them.

It didn't take too long before the three of them were seated in a booth in the café. The café was an attractive place with pink bougainvillea flowers painted on one wall, majestic tupelo trees rising out of sunlit waters on another wall and the colorful storefronts of Main Street on a third wall.

It was also the most popular place in town. It was where everyone came for good food at a reasonable price and, most important of all, the latest gossip.

"Good morning, ladies." Sunny Herbert greeted them with a warm smile. Angelique knew the blonde waitress and Dominique were close friends. "You don't get enough of this place working here?" she teased Dominique.

"Unfortunately, this is the only place in town to get a good breakfast," Dominique replied.

"Good answer," Sunny said with another one of her bright smiles. "So, what can I get for you all?"

The three placed their orders. Angelique got a cheese omelet, Dominique got the French toast and Monique ordered pancakes. They all got their coffees and then small-talked as they waited for their food to arrive.

Monique worked at a dress boutique in town, and she talked about who had been in and who had bought what in the past couple of days. It was always fun to hear who had shopped and who Monique had made sales to.

As they talked, Angelique was aware of the curious glances that came from the other diners in the place. This was the first time the three of them had been out together in public since their mother's funeral. Of course, they had always garnered curious gazes since they were the voodoo queen's daughters.

Their food arrived and for a couple of minutes they fell silent as they focused on eating. They were halfway through the meal when Lucinda Reese stopped by their table.

Lucinda was one of the wealthy in town. She was in her sixties and from the top of her perfectly coiffed hair to the bottom of her expensive shoes, she looked like money.

She was one of the clients who Mystique would meet at her house. There was no way a woman like Lucinda could make the trek through the swamp to see the voodoo queen.

"I just wanted to stop by and give you all my sympathies," she said. "Unfortunately, I was out of town on the day of her funeral and didn't get a chance to give my condolences."

"Thank you, Mrs. Reece," Angelique replied.

"Your mother not only helped me with some personal issues, but I also considered her my friend. Anyway, I'll let you get back to your meal now." She didn't wait for a reply, but instead rejoined three other women who were seated at a four-top table nearby.

Angelique knew Daniel had spoken to Lucinda about the murder. There was no way Angelique could believe that the older woman had murdered her mother. But maybe she wanted Mystique's book so nobody would ever know the reason for her visits. Maybe she'd paid somebody to kill Mystique and steal the book.

Aware of her thoughts leading her down a dark road, she focused again on the conversation her sisters were having.

The rest of the meal went by with no more interruptions. They finished up and paid and left a nice tip for Sunny, then they got back in the car and headed home.

"We all agreed we'd let you be the voice for all of us as far as the investigation went. So, what have you heard from Chief LeCroix?" Monique asked from the back seat as Angelique was driving them home.

She filled them in on what Daniel and his team had been doing for the past week and then brought up the missing book. "Is it possible Mama carried it to one of your homes and she accidentally left it there?"

"I've seen the book in Mama's bedroom before, but I don't think I have it at my house," Dominique said. "But I'll look around to make sure it isn't there."

"I don't think I have it, either," Monique added.

"Is it possible whoever killed Mama took the book?" Dominique asked.

"I think it's very possible," Angelique replied. "Anyway, you're all caught up now, and I'll let you know what's happens with the investigation as it goes on."

By that time, they were back at the swamp entrance. Angelique parked and they got out of the car and headed into the thick vegetation they all called home.

When they reached Monique's shanty, Angelique gave her youngest sister a big hug. Monique clung to her for a long moment and then the two released each other. "Call me tomorrow?" Angelique said.

"I will," Monique replied. "I'll see you both later."

When Monique disappeared into her shanty, Dominique and Angelique continued walking on. "I worry about her," Angelique said. "She's not as emotionally strong as we are."

"Mama babied her a lot," Dominique replied. "She'll have to grow up fast now."

"I still worry about her," Angelique replied.

"She'll be fine," Dominique said. "We're all survivors, sis."

By that time, they had reached Dominique's home. The two hugged, and then Angelique continued on her way. It was always good when the three sisters got together. There had never been any sibling rivalry between them; rather they had always been the best of friends.

It was a little after eleven when Angelique walked back into her shanty. She went directly to the back porch and got her generator running, then went back inside and set up her laptop on the kitchen table.

She needed to work for a few hours. When Angelique had decided she wanted a storefront that would sell natural cures that came from the plants and flowers in the swamp, she knew she needed a way to make money.

Much of her time was spent learning from her mother, but she needed a real job she could do at home at various hours of the day. So she had gone through an online course for medical transcribing.

She now worked three afternoons a week for five doctors in town. She would have worked full-time, but on the other two days another woman took over the job. She and the other woman easily coordinated together and so it worked well for both of them.

It didn't take her long to lose herself in the work. She finished up at five and then closed the computer and focused on making dinner.

Thankfully, the day before she had gone to the grocery store, so she now had a fully stocked cooler and plenty of fruits and vegetables in the bins.

She got out her cooktop and then pulled a piece of fish from her cooler. Fried fish and a salad sounded good, so that's what she fixed.

She ate and cleaned up the mess and then made sure everything was ready for Daniel's evening visit. It was when she was putting on a little extra mascara that she stopped herself and wondered what in the heck she was doing?

Daniel coming to see her certainly wasn't a date. It wasn't a social call at all. She dropped the mascara back into the case where she kept what little makeup she wore and then headed back into the living room.

She grabbed the hardback notebook that sat on the coffee table and opened it. She had decided to write down all the things she'd learned from her mother about swamp plants and flowers and their medicinal uses.

It would be her bible of sorts in moving forward with her plans to open a shop and try to help the people both in the swamp and in town.

Tomorrow, she intended to head out into the swamp in an effort to find the places where those plants and flowers grew. Her mother had taken her out many times to gather the vegetation she needed and to show Angelique where to gather them, but Angelique would need to find the plants and flowers on her own now.

Angelique was trying to stay busy so her mind wouldn't take her back to that moment when she'd found her mother in her bed with her throat gaping open. It was a horrendous vision that haunted her, and she knew it would continue to haunt her for years to come.

It was just after nine when her phone rang and it was Daniel. “I’m sorry, but I’m not going to be able to make it out there tonight. I’ve got a late-night interview, but I’ll fill you in on everything tomorrow night.”

“Okay, I understand,” she replied even as a wave of disappointment swept through her.

“I promise I’ll be there tomorrow night unless something vital comes up,” he replied.

“Then I’ll just see you tomorrow night,” she replied. They said their goodbyes and then she hung up. Was she disappointed that she wasn’t getting an update on the case or because she wouldn’t be seeing Daniel again? She didn’t even want to examine the answer to that.

Instead, she decided to go on to bed. She went outside and turned off the generator, then went back inside and changed into her nightshirt. She made sure the doors were locked and then got into bed.

The sounds of the swamp that drifted in comforted her. It was a lullaby of croaking bullfrogs and the click and whir of insects. Rhythmic waves lapped against the stilts that held the shanty up and occasionally a splash of a fish jumping in the water could be heard.

She must have drifted off to sleep for she awakened suddenly. She bolted upright, her heart racing as fight-or-flight adrenaline raced through her.

What was going on? What had pulled her from her sleep so suddenly? Had it been a bad dream? She drew in and released several deep breaths. Moonlight drifted into the bedroom window and she looked around the room. Everything appeared to be just as it should be.

Maybe it had been a dream and nothing more. She drew in more deep, long breaths as she began to relax once again and her heart slowed its frantic pace.

Then she heard it…the unmistakable tinkle of breaking glass. It came from the living room.

Instantly her heart beat wildly as a new hot adrenaline shot through her veins. Slowly, quietly, she slid out of the bed. She paused and listened. She released a soft gasp as she felt a sudden shift in the air pressure.

Somebody was in her shanty.

She paused just inside the bedroom door. Soft footsteps sounded against the floor as they came closer to her bedroom. Who? Who was out there?

Was it her mother's murderer coming back for her? A cold chill slithered up her spine. Terror rose in the back of her throat, making it difficult for her to draw a deep breath.

She didn't have a weapon, but had no intention of just standing and letting whatever danger was out there come to her. At least she had the element of surprise on her side. The person wouldn't know that she had awakened.

Drawing in a deep breath, she whirled out of the bedroom. In the moonlight that drifted in through the windows she had only a moment to process that the intruder was dressed all in black and wore a ski mask.

It was only when Angelique rushed toward the person that she saw the glint of a knife in the intruder's gloved hands. She halted in her tracks. "Who are you and what do you want?" she demanded.

There was no answer other than the person stepping closer to Angelique. The person jabbed out with the knife, and Angelique danced sideways to keep from getting cut.

Frantically she thought of the room and what could be used as a weapon. She screamed in pain as the knife slashed her arm. She kicked out in an effort to keep the attacker at bay. Another swipe of the knife slashed her once again on her arm.

Again, Angelique kicked her legs, hoping to catch the intruder with a solid blow. As she kicked, she slowly moved toward the potbellied stove in the corner of the room.

It was obvious the trespasser intended to stab her to death. Without a weapon of her own, her death was a very strong possibility. The fear inside her was a living, breathing entity. She also knew any screams for help she released would go unheard as the nearest shanty was too far away.

Once she was backed up against the stove, she fumbled in the darkness and released a deep gasp of relief as her fingers closed around the fireplace poker.

She pulled it up and out and wielded it like a sword, slashing it through the air and successfully backing up the intruder. The knife was sharp, but the poker was long and sturdy. As if knowing the balance of power was now in Angelique's favor, the person turned and ran out the front door.

Angelique ran to the door, slammed it shut and

locked it. However, she immediately saw that the window next to the door was broken. Once the window was broken, all the person had to do was reach in, unlock the door and walk right in, which was obviously what he or she had done.

None of that mattered now as fear continued to half choke her and blood ran down her arm from the two slashing wounds she'd sustained.

The police. She ran to the bedroom and grabbed her cell phone off the nightstand and then returned to the living room with the poker still in her hand. She needed the police here. She needed…she wanted Daniel here as soon as possible.

She called his number and he answered on the first ring. "LeCroix," he said.

"Daniel, somebody just broke into my shanty and attacked me," she said and then burst into tears.

Chapter Four

Daniel's heart beat wildly as he got into his patrol car and headed for the swamp. Two patrol cars and an ambulance followed him as he raced to get to Angelique.

He had heard the raw fear in her tearful, quivering voice. The only information he'd gotten was that she was safe at the moment. It was two o'clock in the morning, and thank God the streets were empty, letting him speed faster than he normally would.

Why would somebody attack Angelique? Was this somehow tied to her mother's murder? Why had Mystique been murdered? Who would have a beef with Mystique's daughter?

He tightened his grip on his steering wheel as a wave of deep frustration swept through him. But the main emotion that rose inside him was a deep, nearly overwhelming concern for Angelique.

Finally, they arrived at the swamp's entrance and Daniel quickly exited his car. There were three night duty cops with him as well as the two EMTs. They all had heavy-duty flashlights, and they quickly began the trek into Angelique's place with Daniel in the lead.

Daniel moved fast, needing to get to Angelique as quickly as possible. He heard the others struggling to keep up, but that didn't make him slow down.

The fact that she'd called told him she was safe, but he had no idea if she'd been hurt. A deep worry pressed tight against his chest. Dammit, he should have asked her more questions while he'd had her on the phone, but she'd been crying so hard and his only thought had been to get to her as soon as possible.

Finally, the shanty came into view. Light spilled out the front window, a window where a pane by the front door appeared to be broken. He raced across the bridge and to the door. It was locked. "Angelique, it's me...open the door. It's me, Daniel."

The door flew open and she stood before him. She was achingly pale and clad in a hot pink nightshirt. She had a white-knuckle hold on a fireplace poker. Her eyes were tear filled and blood ran down one of her arms. She appeared to be in a state of shock.

"Angelique, give me the poker," he said softly. "Give me the poker, honey."

She looked at the poker as if she'd never seen it before. She held it out to him and then began to cry once again. He handed the poker to Jeffrey Cookingham, one of the night duty officers, then he took Angelique by her elbow and led her to the sofa.

"It's okay...you're safe now," he said softly and motioned for the two EMTs to approach her. "Angelique, I see you're hurt on your arm. Do you have any other injuries?"

She drew in a deep breath and released it on a shuddery sigh. "No, it's just my arm."

Linda Farrow, one of the EMTs knelt in front of Angelique and then opened the first aid kit she'd carried in with her.

While Linda cleaned up the two cuts, Daniel directed his officers to head outside and check the area for any signs of the intruder, and then he began to question Angelique.

"Tell me exactly what happened?" he asked gently.

His blood chilled as she told him about awakening to the sound of breaking glass. If she hadn't heard that, if she hadn't awakened when she did, then she probably would have been dead…stabbed to death in her sleep.

"Was it a male or a female?" he asked.

"I just assume it was a man." She winced as Linda cleaned out the wounds with alcohol.

"Are you certain it was a man?" he asked.

She released a tremulous sigh. "No, right now I'm not sure about anything."

"Can you guess height…weight?"

She frowned. "I'm sorry, I don't know. It was so dark and everything happened so fast. All I know is the person was dressed all in black and wore a ski mask and gloves."

"Is there anyone you can think of who might want to harm you?"

"No, nobody I can think of. I spend much of my time either here or in the swamp alone or with my sisters," she replied. "I honestly can't think of anyone who might want me dead." She looked down at her arm where Linda was applying antibiotic cream.

Linda smiled up at her. "You were lucky, Miss Santori. The wounds aren't too deep and I don't believe you need any stitches. I'll just bandage them up, and then in a couple of days you need to reapply the antibiotic cream and then bandage them up for another few days."

"Thank you," Angelique replied.

As Linda and her partner Ramone left the shanty, all three of the officers checked in, stating they had found nothing unusual outside.

"Do you have any wood that we can use to board up the broken window?" Daniel asked her.

"Actually, there are several planks of wood in a variety of sizes on my back deck," she replied. "They were left over when Mama had the deck built."

"Do you have a hammer and some nails?"

"I do. I'll just get them for you. They're in the kitchen," she replied. She got up from the sofa and Daniel and Officer Adam Kincaid followed her.

Minutes later a piece of plywood was in place over the broken piece of glass in the window. Once that was done, the men checked all around the living room, where the fight had taken place. They looked for any kind of evidence that might help to identify the intruder, but unfortunately found nothing.

Once that was done, Daniel dismissed his officers and they left to resume their nightly duties on the streets of Dark Waters. Under normal circumstances Daniel would have had them attempt to lift prints from the front door lock and knob. But Angelique had told him the perpetrator had worn gloves, so there was really no point.

Alone with Angelique, he sat down next to her on the sofa. Thankfully some of the color had returned to her face and she appeared calmer and more collected than she had been when they first arrived.

He couldn't help himself. Although it wasn't very professional, he took her hand in his. Her cold fingers immediately curled around his as if seeking his warmth.

"How are you doing?" he asked. He wanted to pull her into his arms and feel her heart beating against his. He wanted to hold her tight and assure himself she was really okay. This could have been a nightmare and she could have easily wound up dead.

"I'm doing better than I was when you first arrived," she replied. "I'm afraid and I'm angry. I'm also utterly confused as to who attacked me and why."

"I'm going to do my very best to get you those answers," he replied. "In the meantime, I need you to think of anyone who might have a grudge against you, anyone you might have had words with in the last month or so, no matter how insignificant it seemed at the moment."

"Trust me, I'll be thinking about that until we figure this out," she replied.

"There's no *we* in this investigation. Angelique, I want you to think about it, but there's no way I want you going off on your own to find answers," he said firmly.

She offered him a half smile. "Now, why on earth would you think I'd do such a thing?"

A small laugh escaped him. "You know exactly why I would think such a thing."

Her smile fell away and she appeared small and vulnerable once again. "Trust me, I'll cooperate with you in any way I can, but I intend to leave the investigation up to you."

"That's my girl," he replied. He squeezed her hand and then released it and stood. "Now, do you want to go to one of your sisters'? If so, I'll wait for you to pack a bag or whatever, and then I'll walk you out."

She stood as well. "I'm not going to one of my sisters' places or anywhere else. I'm not going to allow some creep to chase me out of my home. Trust me, I won't be caught unaware again. Mama had a knife she kept for protection, and that knife will be my new best friend and bedmate from now on."

She raised her chin and for a moment she looked like a strong, beautiful warrior. A wave of renewed attraction to her filled him.

"My back door has a good lock on it and now with the board in place nobody will be able to reach a hand in to unlock my front door. I'll be just fine here." She offered him another one of her half smiles. "It's late, Daniel. Go home, and I'll just see you tomorrow night."

"If you're sure?"

"I'm positive," she assured him.

Together they walked to the front door. He was reluctant to leave her here all alone, but there was really nothing else he could do. He didn't have the manpower to put a guard on her and at least for now the danger had passed.

When they reached the door, he turned back to look at her.

She was still clad in the pink nightshirt that now was stained with blood on one side from her wounds. Thank God she had only been sliced on her arm. It could have been so much worse. It could have been deadly.

She looked like a victim until he looked into her eyes. There was a strength there in the gorgeous light brown depths, and a deep admiration for her filled him.

He reached out and pushed a strand of her hair away from her face. She took a step closer to him, bringing with her the scent that half dizzied his senses.

For a long moment they stood intimately close to each other. A snap of energy filled the air and her lush lips parted as if in invitation of a kiss. Damn, he really wanted to kiss her, but in the back of his mind a voice of reason finally moved him a step away from her.

"Good night, Angelique. Call me if you need me for anything, and I mean anything. And keep thinking about who the attacker might have been. In the meantime, I'll see you tomorrow evening," he said.

"I'll be here." Her eyes appeared to darken. "I only have one request…if possible could you not tell my sisters about this attack on me tonight? The last thing I want to do is worry them."

He frowned. "I'm sorry, but I can't keep that request. To do my job right I need to speak with both of them. One of them might have valuable information about the reason for the assault on you tonight. Unfortunately, I will be talking to them tomorrow."

She sighed. "All right, I understand. Then I'll just see you tomorrow evening."

They said their goodbyes, and then Daniel stepped out of the shanty. It was after four in the morning and the swamp was relatively quiet as he clicked on his flashlight and began to walk toward the entrance where his car was parked.

As he walked, his brain whirled with dozens of questions. Who had attacked Angelique tonight? And why? Angelique didn't seem the type to go around and cause trouble, but somebody had come after her tonight with a killing rage.

Did this have something to do with Mystique's murder? It seemed damned coincidental that one woman was murdered, and then within weeks her daughter was attacked. Did somebody have a vendetta against the whole Santori family?

Unfortunately, he had to talk to Angelique's sisters, if for no other reason than to warn them of potential danger. If somebody was after the Santori family, then they needed to know they might be in danger, too.

By the time he reached his car, he was exhausted from the night's events and was still very concerned about Angelique's safety. He hated that she was all alone in the shanty.

He didn't even want to think about that moment when they'd stood so close to each other. He especially didn't want to think about how much he'd wanted to kiss her, because he knew if the opportunity presented itself again, he would definitely take it.

ANGELIQUE SLEPT UNTIL after nine the next morning. It had taken her a very long time to fall asleep after Daniel had left. She was aware of each creak and every groan that the shanty made. What had always comforted her now sounded suspicious and had kept her awake. It was around dawn when sleep finally caught up with her.

Once awake, she went about her normal routine, dressing and then starting the generator. As she went about her business, she tried not to think about what had happened the night before, but she couldn't help that her thoughts kept taking her there.

The cuts on her arm were certainly a reminder of what had happened the night before. They burned and hurt. However, she was thankful they hadn't been worse.

There was no question that the intruder had wanted to kill her, or at the very least, greatly harm her. Why? What had she done to somebody to warrant this kind of hatred?

The only places she had been since her mother's funeral were the café with her sisters and the grocery store. Several people had come up to her in the store to give their condolences, and she thought she'd been gracious and kind to each of them. Had she said something off to anyone? She didn't believe so and, in any case, she couldn't believe a simple exchange in the grocery store would result in a murder attempt.

Equally as confusing was that moment just before Daniel had left, when she'd found herself standing so close to him at the front door. There had been a single, breathless moment when she thought he was going to kiss her. And the confusing thing was she had wanted his kiss.

Afraid that he was going to speak to her sisters, she called each of them to let them know what had happened the night before. She tried to downplay it, but both of her sisters were appalled by the attack and each of them offered to put her up until Daniel and his officers figured out who was responsible.

However, she was adamant that she was staying put. She was certain nobody could get in her back door, and as long as the board remained in place over the front window, she didn't believe anyone could get into her front door again.

She felt safe once again in the shanty, and besides, she was still hunting for her mother's book, hoping it would turn up someplace inside her home.

She did find the knife that her mother carried for self-defense in the third bedroom on the shelf. It had a handle with a purple unicorn on it and a blade that was about five inches long. The knife hadn't helped her mother on the night of her murder, but maybe it would help Angelique protect herself in the case of another attack.

She spent the afternoon working and knocked off at five o'clock. At least when she worked, she could only focus on the tasks at hand, which required her complete attention.

Then she took some time and thoroughly searched the little room where her mother would meet her clients. She looked behind everything on the bookcase and around on the floor, but there was no book there to be found.

For dinner, she breaded some shrimp and then fried it up. She also added some broccoli and carrots and made a creamy garlic sauce. It had just finished cooking when a knock sounded on her door.

"Who is it?" she called through the door.

"It's me, Angelique," the familiar deep voice called back.

She opened the door, surprised that Daniel had come so early in the evening. "Come in," she said, noting the very pleasant scent of him as he swept past her. "You're here early this evening."

Tonight, he was out of uniform and looked extremely hot in a pair of jeans and a light blue T-shirt that displayed bulging biceps and his broad shoulders. As usual, he filled the entire space with his energy and complete masculinity.

"I knocked off a little early today," he replied.

"Last night was a late one for you," she said.

"For both of us," he agreed.

"I was just about to eat. Would you like to join me?" she asked. "I have enough to share."

"No thanks, I just had a burger a little while ago. But you go ahead and eat. If you don't mind, I'll sit at the table with you."

They sat at the small table in the kitchen area and

faced each other. He gestured toward her plate. "That definitely looks good. Do you like to cook?"

"Sometimes I enjoy it," she replied. "Lately not as much. It's no fun to cook just for yourself. But I cooked for Mama and me on most nights."

"Do you have any kind of a specialty dish?"

"I've never thought about it before, but I think I make a really good fried fish. I use my own breading and spice concoction and I've been told it's really scrumptious."

"Sounds good. I'd like to try it some time," he replied.

"How about tomorrow night?" she asked impulsively. "If you can get off and be here around six or so, then I'll make you my fish for dinner."

He smiled at her, the gesture crinkling the outer corners of his eyes and causing a pleasant warmth to rush through her. "I will definitely try to be here for that."

"What about you? Do you cook?" she asked. This was the first time they weren't talking about murder and mayhem, and she was enjoying the strictly social conversation. There would be time enough later to talk about what he'd done today in his professional capacity.

He laughed. "I guess you could call it that. If it comes in a box and is microwavable, it's my friend. I eat a lot of burgers and I have a lot of my dinners in the café."

"Then I'll definitely fix you a nice, home-cooked meal tomorrow night," she replied. It didn't mean anything, she told herself. She was just doing a favor for the man who was working hard for her and her sisters.

"That sounds great," he replied. "Now, you eat. You're letting your dinner get cold."

"I'll just warm it up later. Why don't we go on into the living room."

"Are you sure? I didn't mean to interrupt your meal," he replied with a frown.

"It's okay," she said and assured him with a smile. "To be honest, I'm not really that hungry right now anyway."

It took them only moments to settle in on the sofa. Several lanterns were lit because the board on the window kept the sunlight from coming in.

He sat close enough to her that she could feel the body heat wafting from him, she could smell the scent that stirred her and created that crazy pool of warmth deep inside her.

She wasn't sure what it was about the handsome lawman, but something about him made her feel especially feminine and pretty. Maybe he would be the first man she'd take as a lover…no strings attached. It would just be a hook-up without commitment.

She chided herself, wondering where that thought had come from. It was crazy. She didn't really know him at all, and in any case her heart was still broken from her experience with Jason Webber. It was forever broken and she wasn't the least bit interested in having any kind of a romantic relationship.

"How did you spend your day?" he asked.

"I worked for most of the afternoon," she replied.

He gazed at her with obvious curiosity. "What do you do for work?"

"I'm a medical transcriber. Among other things, I deal with insurance and collections, but that's certainly not my real passion," she said.

"Then what's your real passion?"

"Doing a lot of the work my mother did, only I want to open a storefront in town and sell some of the natural remedies that come from the swamp," she replied.

"So, you want to become the next voodoo queen?" he asked with a teasing sparkle in his eyes.

She laughed. "Not hardly, and despite what some people think, my mother wasn't a voodoo queen, although I'll admit she sometimes liked to play the part. Really, she just wanted to help people."

"I've spoken to several people in town and in the swamp who have spoken very highly of your mother and the help they received from her."

"That's nice to hear. Anyway, that's my goal. The medical transcribing is just a means to an end."

"How long before you get that storefront?"

"I'm hoping within the next couple of weeks or so," she replied. "People don't realize how healing some of the plants and flowers from the swamp can be."

She leaned forward as she continued, "For instance black willow bark is an anti-inflammatory and can help treat arthritis and gout, among other things. The stems and leaves of jewelweed are used to relieve itching and pain from hives and poison ivy. Several parts of the groundsel bush help treat fever and congestion and chills."

She sat back, realizing she had gone off on a tangent of sorts. "I'm so sorry, I must be boring you to death."

"Not at all," he said. "Actually, I find it all quite fascinating."

She narrowed her eyes. "Are you lying to me, Chief LeCroix?"

He laughed, the low deep sound pleasant to her ears. "No. I don't lie. I might have my flaws, but lying isn't one of them. My officers will tell you I'm always brutally honest."

"All men lie," she replied as a small shaft of pain stabbed through her. Certainly Jason had lied to her. He'd lied every time he'd told her that he loved her. He'd lied to her every time he encouraged her with their talks of a wonderful future together.

"If you really believe that, then it's a damned shame," he replied soberly. "Now, unfortunately I had to speak with your sisters today. I needed to get their take on who might have attacked you."

"What did you learn from them?"

"Damn little," he replied. "Neither one of them could think of anyone who might want to attack you. Have you had any more thoughts about it?"

"I've thought about it all day long, but I still can't think of anyone who would want me dead." A sudden shiver walked up her spine as she thought about the attack that had happened. Thank God she had awakened when she had. If she hadn't, there was no question in her mind that she would be dead. She touched one of the bandages on her arm.

"Do they hurt?" he asked softly.

"A little," she admitted.

"Maybe we should have called the doctor for some pain meds for you," he said.

"I wouldn't have taken them. I'll be fine. They're going to hurt for a little while, but eventually they'll heal up just fine," she replied.

"I can't wait to catch the creep who did that to you," he said, his bright blue eyes slightly narrowed. "But right now, I'll confess that I'm pretty much at a dead end concerning your assault. However I'll continue digging into it until we find the person responsible."

He then went on to tell her the people he'd interviewed concerning her mother's murder. So many questions and still no definitive answers. "Pierre is still at the top of my suspect list, but unfortunately, right now, I don't have enough evidence against him to make an arrest."

"Maybe you should talk to Jacque LeBlanc," she said.

He frowned. "Who is he?"

"He's a gator hunter. He's kind of a mysterious guy. Nobody in the swamp knows very much about him, but it's rumored that he knows a lot about what goes on around here."

"How do I find this guy?" he asked.

"I'm not sure. I know he's friendly with George, so George might know where he lives. It's just a thought," she said and reached up to tuck a strand of hair behind her ear.

"I'll definitely check him out and see if he knows

anything about the murder or about the attack on you," Daniel replied. "And that's where we're at right now."

"I still haven't found the book of Mama's. I'm really starting to believe it was taken by whoever killed her, although I can't imagine why anyone would want it."

"I'm requesting a search warrant for Pierre's shanty. When we went to speak to him before, we stepped inside. But we need to tear the place apart. If the book is there, then that might be enough evidence to bring charges against him. Now you're all caught up with where we are."

"Thank you, Daniel. I appreciate you checking in each evening," she replied. Surprisingly she'd come to look forward to his nightly visits. Certainly, she wanted to be updated on where the investigations stood, but tonight she had enjoyed the strictly social talk they'd had.

Then there was the wild physical attraction she had to him. It was an attraction she hadn't felt for a man in a very long time.

"I'll just get out of here and leave you to the rest of your evening," he said and stood from the sofa. She rose as well and walked with him to the front door.

When they reached it, he turned back to her. Once again, she found herself standing far too close to him. Her heart stepped up its rhythm and even though her brain told her to take a step back from him, she remained in place.

"Are we still on for fried fish tomorrow night?" he asked.

"Absolutely," she replied.

His gaze seemed to be trained on her lips. "Angelique, I have a wild and crazy desire to kiss you."

"I have a wild and crazy desire to let you kiss me," she replied half breathlessly.

He gathered her into his arms and then his mouth claimed hers. Flames of desire instantly swept through her as his lips plied hers with a fiery heat. She opened her mouth to allow him to deepen the kiss.

Their tongues swirled together in a heated dance, and she raised her arms to encircle his neck as he pulled her closer and closer still to him. Their bodies fit together perfectly.

The kiss continued for several long, breathtaking moments, and then he finally released her and took a step backward. There was a hunger still burning in his eyes as he held her gaze.

"That was completely inappropriate," he said, his voice a bit huskier than usual.

"I don't agree," she countered. "What was inappropriate about it? What's wrong with two single, consenting adults sharing a kiss?"

He frowned and raked a hand through his thick, dark hair. "It…it just doesn't feel right, given our positions."

"It had nothing to do with our positions," she replied. "You're a man and I'm a woman, and it simply had to do with the fact that we wanted to kiss each other."

He grinned then. "You are one stubborn woman. Do you ever lose an argument?"

"Rarely," she replied with a smile of her own. "Now, good night, Daniel, and I'll see you tomorrow night."

"Good night, Angelique." With that, he turned and walked out into the darkness of the swamp. She closed and locked the door and then raised a hand to her lips, where the imprint of his very hot lips still lingered.

She then went back into the kitchen to eat the meal she'd fixed for herself. She warmed it up in a saucepan and then ate. Once she was finished, she cleaned the dishes and then went outside to shut off her generator.

She stood for a few minutes at her railing and watched the near-full moon play on the water. As usual, it was absolutely beautiful. The tall trees on the bank were reflected in the water and it was picture-perfect.

However, it wasn't long before the hair on the back of her neck rose and a deep sense of disquiet filled her. She looked around the area, but saw nothing and nobody. Still, she felt as if somebody was watching her and waiting for the perfect opportunity to strike again.

Chapter Five

Daniel left Angelique's with the kiss they'd shared in the forefront of his mind. Her lips had been so soft, so pillowy and luscious. She had tasted delicious and he could have kissed her for hours if a little part of his brain hadn't intervened.

Had it been wrong to kiss her? She certainly didn't believe so. Still, the last thing he wanted to do was somehow take advantage of her. Was it her need for answers from him that made her kiss him so passionately?

He didn't have the answer to that, and in any case even though he'd love to kiss her again, he was determined to rein in his attraction to her. Surely it was best to keep things strictly professional between them. Blurring the lines wasn't a good idea. Still, he'd like to know what man had made her believe that all men lied.

By the time morning came, he was once again immersed in the two cases...one a murder and one an attempted murder. He contacted Judge Waylan Frankel to get a search warrant for Pierre Guidry's shanty. The judge wasn't in but his clerk took the message, and Daniel hoped to get the warrant before the end of the day.

At nine, with the sun bright overhead, Daniel took Clay and Luke with him back to the swamp in search of the elusive Jacque LeBlanc, the gator hunter who Angelique had told him about.

Their first stop was at George's place to see if they could get directions to Jacque's shanty. "To be honest, I don't know exactly where Jacque lives. We usually meet up at an old cypress tree down that way," George said.

He pointed to a narrow trail Daniel had never been on before. "If you take that, you'll eventually come to a fork. Take the left path and you'll come up on the huge tree. You can't miss it, and I would guess he lives someplace right around there."

"Thanks, George. Hopefully we can find him," Daniel replied.

The three men headed up the path where brush, vines and tree roots encroached. It was a hot day and humidity hung thick as mosquitoes and other insects buzzed lazily in the air.

They came to the fork in the path and went to the left, where the path was even narrower. Delicate spiderwebs hung in the bushes and trees they passed and appeared to sparkle in the sunlight that managed to peek through the leaves overhead.

Small animals ran on either side of the path, and in a large pool of water they passed several alligators gliding in the dark depths.

They finally came to a huge bald cypress tree. There

was no question that this was the tree George had mentioned to them. It rose majestically on the side of a still pool of water, far bigger than the others nearby.

They continued on the path and eventually came to a sturdy-looking shanty tucked deep within the overgrown wilderness. "Jacque LeBlanc," Daniel yelled out.

He had no idea if this was the right place or not. He was about to holler once again when the door opened and a tall, well-built man stepped out on the porch. "Jacque LeBlanc?"

"Who's asking?"

"I'm Chief of Police Daniel LeCroix and these are two of my men, Officers Caldwell and Madison," Daniel said. "We'd like to talk to you."

"About?"

"Mystique Santori's murder," Daniel replied.

"You might as well come on in," Jacque said and opened his door wide.

The inside of Jacque's shanty was a bit of a shock. Not only was it neat and clean, but there was a large bookcase against one wall filled with books about a variety of subjects.

Jacque himself was also a bit of a surprise. His dark hair was long and tied at the nape of his neck like most of the men in the swamp. He was clean-shaven and clad in jeans and a navy-blue short-sleeved button-down shirt. He wore the air of the city about him instead of the swamp.

"Please, have a seat." He gestured them to the dark

gray sofa, while he sat in the matching chair facing them. "Now, what can I do for you?"

"Tell us what you know about Mystique Santori's murder," Daniel said.

Jacque sat back in the chair and raised a dark brow. "What makes you think I know anything about it?"

"Angelique Santori told us you know a lot about what goes on here in the swamp," Daniel explained.

"I try to keep my ear to the ground," Jacque replied.

"So, have you heard anything that might help us solve this murder?" Daniel leaned forward, hoping… praying that the man might know something that would be useful to their investigation.

"I can tell you Mystique's death shook up most of the people around here. Some of them feared she was powerful enough to come back to life and worried that she would come back filled with a vengeance," Jacque said. "Most everyone in the swamp was afraid of Mystique."

"Were you afraid of her?" Daniel asked curiously.

Jacque's green eyes appeared to darken. "No, I'm not afraid of anything. Besides, I met Mystique one night not too long ago. I was fishing in a small pool of water and she was out looking for a particular kind of flower that only opened at night. She surprised me by sitting next to me on the bank and we chatted for about an hour."

"Did she say anything that might help us find her killer?" Daniel asked.

"No, although she did complain about her man, Pierre Guidry. She said she was done with him. She was tired of their constant bickering. She mostly talked about her daughters and how much she loved them. Oh, she did mention that somebody was irritated with her because a love spell didn't work."

"Charles Lathrop," Luke murmured.

"Anything else you can tell us?" Daniel asked.

Jacque shook his head. "I'm sorry I don't have more to tell you."

"There was an attack on Angelique. Do you know anything about that?"

"No, I haven't heard anything about that."

Daniel stood, and Clay and Luke also got up from the sofa. "I appreciate you speaking with us. Can you continue to keep your ear to the ground and let us know if you hear anything that might help us out in our investigation?"

Jacque also rose to his feet. "I can do that. Why don't you give me your cell phone number? I don't go into town much, but I can give you a call if I hear anything that might be useful to you."

It took only moments for the two to exchange numbers, and then the three lawmen left the shanty. They didn't speak until they got back to the car.

"Interesting guy," Luke said as Daniel drove back toward town.

"Did you see all those books? I've never known a gator hunter who is a big reader before," Clay said.

"I have a feeling Jacque isn't swamp born and raised. I should have asked him how long he's been there and where he came from, not that any of that matters," Daniel replied. "One thing is for certain,

Charles Lathrop just moved right up there with Pierre as a suspect."

"I didn't like that guy the first time we talked to him," Luke said. "I thought he was very arrogant and more than a little bit creepy."

"Yeah, it's no wonder the man needed a love spell," Clay added. "And apparently even that didn't work for him."

"We'll see if he's a killer as well as an arrogant creep," Daniel replied.

The afternoon passed quickly as the search warrant for Pierre's place came through and after the search was completed, Daniel requested a search warrant for Charles Lathrop's home. Nothing of interest was found at Pierre's, so Daniel was hoping they would find something at Charles's house.

As they waited for that search warrant to come through, the three of them sat in the conference room dedicated to the murder and not only tossed out ideas about Mystique's murder but also the attack on Angelique.

"It's too bad Angelique's sisters couldn't come up with a single suspect for us," Clay said.

"It's too bad Angelique doesn't have a clue as to who wants to harm her," Daniel replied. "It's hard to investigate a case when you don't even know where to start," he added in a frustration that was growing far too familiar.

"Hopefully Angelique scared the person away for good," Luke said.

"I'd like to believe that, but I don't," Daniel replied.

"My biggest fear is that the perp is going to try again, and next time Angelique might not be so lucky."

Once again, his head filled with thoughts of the amazingly hot kiss they had shared. Kissing Angelique could definitely become addictive if he let it.

There was just something that made him want to know more about her. She'd shared a little bit about herself the night before, but it hadn't been nearly enough to satisfy his curiosity.

Of course, in the end it all meant nothing. She was just a beautiful woman who intrigued him, and more importantly, she was the victim in two crimes. But she really wasn't his type and, in any case, he had no time for romance. He had a murder and an attempted murder to solve.

He couldn't do anything to save Mystique. She was already dead and gone. But somehow, someway he needed to figure out who had attacked Angelique before the person struck again with potentially deadly results.

ANGELIQUE WALKED THROUGH the swamp with her mother's knife held tight in her hand. It was early afternoon, and knowing she was cooking for Daniel tonight, she needed to go to the grocery store and pick up a few things.

She had always felt as if the swamp welcomed her when she walked through the junglelike greenery. Today was no different. A faint breeze rustled through the treetops. Birds called to each other in a sweet chorus overhead as small animals scurried through the brush. In the distance she heard the slap of an alligator's tail against the water.

She had never been afraid here before, but today a new wariness filled her as she walked quickly down the path that would lead her to her car. She kept her gaze focused on the left and the right of the trail with an occasional glance over her shoulder to make sure she wasn't being followed.

Somebody was after her. Somebody had broken into her shanty and had tried to kill her. And there was no reason to believe that the person wouldn't try again. That thought made her grip the knife more firmly in her hand. She had no idea where the danger might come from, which only made it all the more frightening.

She breathed a deep sigh of relief when she finally reached her car. She slid behind the wheel, locked the doors, started the engine and then pulled out in the direction of town.

Last night she had tossed and turned with thoughts of the kiss she had shared with Daniel. It had been so totally unexpected and so totally hot.

The minute he had pulled her into his arms and his lips had claimed hers, she'd had a fire in her belly that she had never felt before. She had immediately been hungry for more from him. He had stirred her with just a kiss; she couldn't even imagine what it would be like to make love with him.

And she shouldn't even be thinking about that. She had more important things to think about, like who might want her dead. She had been racking her brain, trying to think of anyone who might have an issue with her, but she came up empty.

Once she reached town, she decided to stop at the dress shop where Monique worked. All That Jazz was dedicated to pandering to the women in town. It not only sold trendy and classic clothing but also purses, shoes, costume jewelry and bath and perfume items. Monique had been working there for the past three years, and last year had earned the title of assistant manager.

Angelique worried about her baby sister, who, since their mother's murder had become slightly distant and quiet. It was obvious she was still deeply grieving, but chose to do it alone rather than with her two sisters to support her.

A tiny bell tinkled over the door as Angelique walked into the shop. The pleasant scents of lilac and vanilla and a hint of cinnamon with a variety of floral fragrances greeted her.

Monique stood behind the cash register. She was clad in a long, navy skirt and a red-and-navy peasant-style blouse. Her long dark hair was braided down her back and she looked positively lovely.

She offered up a surprised smile at the sight of Angelique. "Hey, sis. I didn't expect to see you in here today," she said as she moved around the counter and then gave Angelique a hug.

"I had to come into town to the grocery store and so I decided to stop in to see you," Angelique replied. "You've been kind of scarce lately."

"I've been working extra hours to keep busy. It's good for me right now to stay busy. The real question is how are you doing?"

"I'm doing okay," Angelique replied lightly. The last thing she wanted to do was worry her baby sister with how much the attack had affected her.

"For real?" Monique looked at her with concern.

"For real," Angelique replied with a laugh. "I'm just rolling with the punches right now."

"Well, let's hope there are no more punches," Monique replied. "On another subject, I spent this morning unpacking and tagging a shipment of new clothes that came in. When I saw one article, I immediately thought of you."

Angelique followed her sister to a rack that held loungewear. Monique pulled out a honey-colored caftan with a V-neck that was lined with tiny pearls. "This would look gorgeous on you."

"I love it. I'll take it," Angelique replied.

Monique laughed. "Wow, that was the easiest sale I've made all month."

"That's because you know exactly what I like. In fact, I'll wear it this evening." That was part of why Monique was so successful as a salesperson. She knew her clientele and how to match women with the clothes.

"Anything special going on this evening?" Monique asked as the two walked back toward the cash register.

"I'm cooking dinner for Chief LeCroix."

Monique raised a dark brow in obvious surprise. "Why?"

"I know how hard he's been working to find answers for us, and he doesn't really ever get a home-cooked meal, so I offered to fry up some of my special fish for him this evening," Angelique replied.

Monique's lips turned up in a half smile. "You like him."

"It's not like that," Angelique replied quickly, even as the memory of his very hot kiss filled her head.

"It is like that," Monique replied with a full grin. "I can see it on your face. You're totally into him."

"Okay, I'll admit I like him a little bit. Of course I don't know him very well, but what I do know about him, I like. But you know it won't go anywhere."

Monique studied her for a long moment as her grin fell. "You know, Angelique, someday you're going to have to get over Jason."

Angelique stiffened. "I'm well over him. I learned all I needed to know about men from him. Anyway, ring me up, sis. It's time I get moving to the grocery store."

The last thing she wanted to do was hang around here and talk about the man who had broken her heart into a million pieces. It was true, she was over him. She just didn't want to allow any man to ever get that close to her again.

A few minutes later she left the shop and headed to her car. She placed the new caftan on her passenger seat and then drove to the grocery store down the block. Howard's Grocery wasn't a huge place, but it was the only grocer in town. Howard Griffin was a big, affable man, who often greeted the shoppers who came in.

"Afternoon, Miss Santori," he said as she walked in.

"Good afternoon to you, Mr. Griffin," she replied.

"Now, I've told you at least a dozen times to call me Howard. I don't stand on formalities around here."

"Then Howard it is," she said with a smile. "And you can call me Angelique."

He grabbed her a cart and pushed it toward her. "Let me know if you can't find something, Angelique," he said. "If I don't have what you need, then I'll order it and I'll have it for you next time you come in."

"Thank you, Howard." She grabbed hold of the basket and pushed it toward the produce section. She needed to grab a few things in order to make coleslaw, which always went well with fish. She also planned to make mac and cheese from scratch. And if she got really ambitious, she'd make some skillet corn bread to round out the meal.

She found herself looking forward to the evening. It was true, she liked what she knew about Daniel and she was looking forward to getting to know him even more. Then there was the crazy physical attraction she felt toward him. It burned hot inside her.

"Angelique." She turned at the sound of her name coming from someplace behind her. She smiled as she saw Marianne Lutgen approaching her.

"Hi, Marianne," she greeted the plump, brown-haired woman. Marianne had grown up in the swamp and she and Angelique had often played together as children. However, they'd grown apart during their teen years.

"I wanted to tell you that I'm having a little gathering tonight at my place, and as usual, I'd love for you to come," Marianne said.

"Oh, I'm sorry, Marianne, I won't be able to make it. I have other plans for the evening, but thank you for the invitation," Angelique replied.

"You're never available when I invite you to do anything. You never come to my parties." Marianne's lower lip jutted out in a pout. "Do you think you're better than me and my friends?"

"Of course not," Angelique replied, appalled that Marianne would even think that about her. "Again, I'm sorry, but my life has been so busy, especially lately."

"Did you know I came to see your mother once?" Marianne said.

"No, I didn't know that," Angelique replied with a bit of surprise.

Marianne grabbed a can of corn from the nearby shelf and tossed it into her basket, then looked at Angelique once again. "I went to see her because I wanted her to do a spell or something that would make me lose some weight."

"I hope she was helpful to you."

"She wasn't," Marianne said flatly. "She told me that if I really wanted to lose weight then I should stop eating so much." Marianne released a deep sigh. "Anyway, I just wanted to tell you about the party tonight. Maybe next time you'll be able to come."

"We'll see," Angelique replied. "In any case it was nice seeing you again, Marianne."

A few minutes later Angelique finished up her shopping, paid and then loaded the groceries into her trunk. It was on her way home when she thought about the brief conversation with Marianne once again.

There were a couple of reasons why Angelique never went to the parties that Marianne hosted. The first reason was because Marianne ran with a rough crowd. The second reason was Angelique had heard that old man Walt Boudreaux brought jugs of his moonshine to the parties and everyone imbibed freely. Angelique had no desire to spend an evening with a bunch of drunks.

Still, the conversation with Marianne played and replayed in her head because of that moment when she'd said that Angelique's mother hadn't helped her. There had been something hard glowing in the depths of Marianne's eyes. It was there for only a minute and then gone.

Was it possible her mother had been murdered by a woman? So far, the investigation had been focused mostly on men. Marianne was a big woman. She would have been capable of overwhelming the much-smaller Mystique.

Or could it have been Marianne who had broken into the shanty and come after Angelique with a knife? Was the woman really that offended that Angelique never went to her parties? She didn't know what to think anymore, but her brain was certainly working overtime.

She would definitely share with Daniel the conversation she'd had with Marianne. Were there other women they might be overlooking? The crime had been so heinous it was hard for her to imagine a woman being capable of it. But she knew women could be evil killers. She saw stories about women killers all the time on the news.

She pulled into her usual parking space just outside the swamp's entrance and then got out of the car. She picked up the bag with the caftan inside and then got the two small shopping bags out of the trunk of her car. She looped the bags over her left hand so she could carry her knife with her right hand.

Since the night of the attack on her, she never went out without the knife. It wasn't much, but in the event of another unexpected assault, it might make the difference between life and death.

As she walked through the tangled paths toward her home, she kept her gaze shooting all around her and her ears focused to catch any sound that might indicate somebody was near her.

She saw it when she reached the bottom of her bridge…a white piece of paper taped to her front door. What now? As she approached, a chill suddenly raced up her spine. Once again, she felt as if somebody was hiding somewhere in the thick woods and watching her.

She looked all around, but saw nobody. Once she reached the front door, she pulled the piece of paper off and read—"YOUR VOODOO MOTHER CAN'T PROTECT YOU NOW."

Quickly, she unlocked her door and went inside. Her heart beat frantically as another chill ran up her back. She relocked the door and then moved to the part of the window that wasn't boarded up.

She peered outside for several long moments as a deep fear squeezed her chest, making it difficult for her to draw a full breath. First the attack on her and now this?

Who had left the note on her door? Who was after her and why? Seeing nothing and nobody, she moved on stiffened legs to the kitchen. She dropped her bags on the table, set the note down and then sank into a chair.

Her heart beat so fast…so hard, it threatened to explode right out of her chest. The note looked like pure rage on paper, the red letters written hard and big and bold.

Dammit, who had written it?

She could only hope that Daniel would bring her some answers when he arrived. And she couldn't wait for him to get here.

Chapter Six

It was another fruitless, frustrating day for Daniel and his team in the cases of Mystique's murder and Angelique's attack. The only bright spot in the day was the anticipation of having dinner with Angelique.

At five o'clock, he left the police station and raced home. Home for Daniel was a two-story, three-bedroom house just off the main drag. He'd bought it three years ago when he'd entertained dreams of a wife and family. Now he was considering selling it, because at thirty-five years old he'd pretty much given up on finding that special woman for him and having children.

The home came with a large wraparound porch and a fenced backyard. It was painted white with teal-colored shutters. Inside was a nice-sized living room and kitchen with a guest bath and a laundry room.

The upstairs consisted of three large bedrooms, a hallway bath and the primary had an en suite bathroom as well. Once he was home, he raced up the stairs and got into the shower.

The warm spray of water revitalized him as it washed away the day's frustrations. Once he was finished showering, he then shaved and dressed in a pair of jeans and a royal-blue polo shirt. He then put on his shoulder holster and added his gun. By then it was time to leave for Angelique's shanty.

He hated that he had nothing to share with her again this evening concerning the investigations. He'd spoken to half a dozen people today, but none of them had any information that would be helpful in moving the investigations forward. She would be extremely disappointed with his lack of progress and he hated disappointing her.

He'd always believed he was a pretty good lawman, but these two cases were definitely humbling him. He'd started having dreams of Mystique in her grave and crying out to him for justice.

The other nightmare he had started suffering from had Angelique running from a dark figure with a knife. In the dream, she called his name over and over again, seeking help from him that he couldn't give her because he was frozen in place. He knew the only way to halt the nightmares was to solve the cases, and that couldn't happen fast enough.

It was right at six o'clock when he knocked on Angelique's door. She opened it and smiled at him. God, she looked gorgeous. She wore a golden caftan that appeared to slide smoothly over her curves. The gown perfectly matched her honey-colored eyes.

"Right on time. I like a man who is punctual," she said as she opened the door wider to admit him.

"Hmm, something smells very good in here," he replied.

"That would be your dinner. Come on in the kitchen. It's ready to eat now. Did you bring your appetite?"

"I did." He was definitely hungry for something, but it wasn't something she was going to put on a plate.

"Have a seat," she said once they reached the kitchen. The table was set with two white plates and silverware. He sat at the chair facing her as she stirred something on the cooktop.

She then opened the cooler and took out a bowl of coleslaw, which she placed in the center of the table. She grabbed the two plates off the table and set them next to the cookstove. Within moments she had them filled and on the table, where she joined him.

"This looks absolutely amazing," he said. The fish pieces were generous on his plate and looked crispy and light. The mac and cheese looked homemade and appeared especially cheesy and the corn bread was golden brown.

"I hope you like mac and cheese," she said. "I didn't even ask you before I put it on your plate."

"It's a mainstay in a bachelor's diet, but nothing I've ever fixed from a box looks as good as this," he replied.

She grinned. "Mine definitely didn't come from a box. Now help yourself to the coleslaw and let's eat before it gets cold."

The fish was delicious, light yet with spices that enhanced the flavor of the white bass. The mac and cheese and coleslaw were perfect side dishes and the corn bread slathered with butter and a little honey was as good as a dessert.

As they ate, they talked about the unusually warm June the area was experiencing and the plans for a big July Fourth celebration in town. She looked so beautiful that he found it hard to focus on the conversation.

Her hair was loose, a gorgeous curtain of shiny darkness that fell around her shoulders. Her thick eyelashes looked impossibly long and her lips…oh those lush lips taunted and teased him.

By the time they finished eating and he helped her clean up the dishes, twilight had begun to fall. They moved into the living room, where she lit the lanterns and then they sank down on the sofa.

"So, tell me about your day," she said.

He frowned. "I'm afraid to tell you that I really have nothing to report on either case. We're waiting for a search warrant to come through for Charles Landry's place. He and Pierre still remain at the top of my very short list of suspects. But right now, I couldn't even make a circumstantial case against either one of them."

He leaned forward, the scent of her wrapping around him.

"As far as your attacker is concerned, we're no closer to figuring out who it is than we were on the night it happened. I'm sorry, Angelique, but right now, the cases have pretty much stalled out."

"Maybe you'll find my mother's book in Charles's house and that will solve the case, although I can't imagine why he or anyone else would want her book."

"Who knows what drives people to do what they do," he replied.

"Well, I have several bits of news to share with

you," she said. "The first is a conversation I had with Marianne Lutgen." Daniel listened with interest as she relayed her talk with Marianne in the grocery store.

"Interesting," Daniel said when she was finished. "So, she not only had a grudge against your mother but also against you because you never go to her parties."

She released what sounded like a slightly nervous laugh. "I can't imagine her coming to kill me just because I don't socialize with her. Who would do that? But my mother is another story. There was definitely something hard and angry in her eyes when she spoke about my mama."

"I will definitely have a chat with her tomorrow and see if she has alibis for both the night of the murder and the attack on you," he said.

She nodded, and then her eyes appeared to darken. "My next bit of news is when I got back here from the grocery there was a piece of paper taped to my front door." In one graceful movement she got up and went to her bookcase, where she grabbed a piece of paper and then returned to the sofa.

She sat closer to him than she had been before and he could feel an edge of fear that emanated from her. She handed him the paper and as he read it, a deep anxiety thudded into the pit of his stomach.

"This implies that the person who wrote it was afraid of your mother, but now that your mother is gone, all bets are off. This also implies that whatever beef they have with you, it's been brewing for a long time," he said as he stared at the bold red letters.

He looked back up at her. Her eyes were slightly

widened and her lips were parted as if to release either a gasp or a scream. It was obvious the note had scared her. Hell, it scared him for her.

"Do you have a plastic bag I can put the note in? Maybe we'll get lucky and get some fingerprints off it."

She nodded and rose from the sofa. She walked into the kitchen and returned a moment later with a plastic baggie in her hand. He took it from her and she sat next to him as he carefully placed the note inside the protective covering.

He then reached out and took her hand in his. Her fingers were icy. "Maybe it's time you think about moving in with one of your sisters," he said. "I don't like the idea of you being here all alone."

"Absolutely not." She snatched her hand back from his. "Why would I bring this kind of danger to my sisters' doorsteps? No, I'm not going anywhere. This is where I belong and this is where I'm staying." She glared at him as if he was personally responsible for it all.

"Hey, I'm not the enemy here," he protested with his hands up in surrender.

Deep color rose into her cheeks. "I'm sorry, Daniel. I know you're just trying to help, but as I've said before, I'm not leaving my home. I think I'm safe here and besides, I have every confidence that you're going to catch this creep quickly."

"I can't do that without your help. What I need you to do is think back into your past. Not just the last month or so, but rather longer ago than that. Maybe a man you dated in the past or a girlfriend you had a falling-out with. Angelique, there's got to be something there, and I can't do anything unless you give me some names."

Tears misted her eyes as she gazed at the note on the coffee table before them. A deep shudder went through her, making her look small and fragile.

Daniel reached out and drew her into his arms. She held herself stiffly against him, and he was about to withdraw his arms from around her when she melted into him.

Daniel tightened his embrace as she buried her face in the hollow of his throat. She didn't cry but rather remained in his arms, her breath warming his neck.

The heady scent of her surrounded him as he rubbed his hand up and down her back. He wanted to comfort her, but he had no words. He needed to assure her, yet had no assurances to offer her. In any case she didn't remain there long.

After several minutes she raised her head and gazed at him. He saw no fear in her eyes, but rather he saw something else…a hunger that called to something wild and unbridled in him.

She parted her lips and he felt if he didn't kiss her at that very moment, he would explode with his need for her. He claimed her lips with his own.

Her arms tightened around his neck as their tongues swirled together and his desire for her spun completely out of control. His lips slid from hers and he kissed down her neck, loving the taste of her skin.

She leaned her head back, granting him full access

to the length of her throat. She gasped with pleasure as he nuzzled her behind her ear.

His mouth found hers once again, and this kiss was just as deep, just as hungry as the last. They kissed until they were both breathless and then she suddenly withdrew her arms from around his neck. He instantly drew back from her, not wanting to offend her with any unwanted advances.

She stood from the sofa and then held a hand out to him. He looked up at her, confused by her action. Her eyes glowed in the illumination from a nearby lantern and what he saw in the honeyed depths was sheer, raw desire.

"Come with me, Daniel," she said in a whisper. "Come with me to my bedroom and make love with me. Please, Daniel…"

He had a single thought that everything was spiraling out of control, and then he stood and placed his hand in hers and everything suddenly seemed right.

She picked up one of the lanterns and then led him into her bedroom. Once there, she placed the lantern on the nightstand, where it created a soft glow around the bed. He took off his holster and gun and set them next to the lantern, and then she stepped closer to him.

Again, he gathered her into his arms and claimed her lips with his. A burning desire filled him, inflaming his blood and scorching any rational thought from his mind.

All he could think of was Angelique and her sweet, hot lips. All he could focus on was the way her breasts felt pressed against his chest and how perfectly their bodies fit together.

His senses were dizzied by the very scent of her, and all he could think about was his desperate need to have her. She broke their kiss and stepped back from him.

He stood before her, his heart thundering in his chest. Had she changed her mind? It was certainly her prerogative…the next move was up to her and he would respect whatever she wanted.

ANGELIQUE HAD NEVER felt as alive as she did in this moment with Daniel's gaze hot on her and her own desire for him coursing rich and powerful through her body. It had been so very long since she'd felt this way. In fact, she wasn't sure she'd ever felt this way before.

She had desired Daniel since the first time he had come to her shanty. It felt right that tonight they acted on the crazy sexual energy that had existed between them. With this thought in mind, she reached down to her knees, grabbed the caftan's silky material in her hands and then pulled it up and over her head.

It dropped like liquid gold at her feet, leaving her clad only in a white lacy bra and white panties. His heated gaze slowly swept the length of her, as potent as a physical touch against her skin.

He pulled his shirt over his head, dropped it to the floor and then reached for her once again, but before she allowed him to embrace her, she plucked at the zipper on his jeans. She wanted him as naked as she was.

He took her hint and quickly pulled off his jeans and took off his socks, leaving him clad only in a pair of navy boxers. His body in the lamplight was absolutely stunning. His chest was firmly muscled and a six-pack of abs added to his wild attractiveness. His legs were sturdy and well shaped, and overall he was a study in perfect masculinity.

This time when he reached for her, she came willingly back into his arms, where they kissed once again. His fingers danced through her hair and then stroked down her bare back. She could tell that he was aroused and that only increased her desire for him.

She was on fire and Daniel was the only person who could put out the flames. Within minutes they were both breathless again. She broke the embrace only long enough to turn down the lilac-colored bedspread. She slid between the sheets and then beckoned him to join her.

He didn't hesitate. He got into the bed and they came together once again. Their near-naked bodies writhed against each other as they shared another searing kiss. Their legs tangled together and she loved the feel of his warm bare skin against her own.

"Angelique, you are so beautiful," he whispered into her ear as he reached behind her to unfasten her bra. It fell off her, and he plucked it away from her and tossed it to the floor on the side of the bed.

His palms immediately covered her breasts, and she gasped with hot pleasure as he dipped his head and licked at first one and then the other of her erect nipples. Electric currents rushed from her nipples to the very center of her.

"Daniel, you're driving me crazy," she whispered feverishly.

He raised his head and grinned at her. "Good," he replied, his blue eyes twin orbs of fevered heat. "And I'm just getting started."

As if to prove that point, he slid one hand down the length of her stomach. Slowly he caressed further down until he reached the top of her panties. He ran his fingers lightly back and forth, teasing her and building a new need in her that was all-consuming. She pulled the panties down, then kicked them off.

Once again, he slid his hand down…down…and then he was there at the very center of her. His fingers found the most sensitive part of her, and they began to dance against her.

Faster and faster they moved and a tension began to build inside her. Higher and higher she climbed, and then she was there, falling over a cliff as wave after wave of her climax washed over her.

She lay utterly boneless for several moments but then she was ready for more. She plucked at the waistband of his boxers. "Take them off, Daniel," she whispered.

She didn't have to ask him twice. He slid the boxers off, and then she encircled his hardness with her fingers. He moaned as she caressed him, moving her hand up and down the velvety length.

His moans excited her. She loved that she was giving him such complete pleasure. Still, it didn't take long before he pushed her hand away and instead positioned himself between her thighs. He gazed down at her and his eyes blazed with blue fire. Then he entered her.

She clung to his shoulders as she arched up to fully receive him. Once he was deep inside her, he leaned down and claimed her lips in a fiery kiss, and a new tension began to build inside her.

Once the kiss ended, he began to move his hips. In and out of her he pumped slow and steadily. She arched up again to meet him thrust for thrust, and it wasn't long before he went faster and he released a deep groan.

Faster and more frantic they moved against each other, and then she was there…at the top of the cliff once again. She tumbled over it, her orgasm crashing through her with a tremendous force.

He moaned once again and found his own release. He stiffened against her and when he was finished, he collapsed on the bed next to her. The only sound in the room was their panting breaths.

Finally, he propped himself up on one elbow and gazed down at her. "Well, this was certainly a big surprise, Miss Santori."

She laughed. "I'm a woman who knows what I want, and tonight I definitely wanted you."

"I certainly hope I delivered," he replied.

She smiled up at him. "Oh, you did, Chief LeCroix. You totally delivered."

He frowned suddenly. "This all happened so fast I didn't even think about birth control."

"Don't worry about it. I'm on the pill, and it's been a very long time since I've been with a man."

"And it's been a long time since I've been with a woman," he said.

"Stay the night with me?" she asked. She didn't even know she was going to ask him this until the words fell out of her mouth. At least for the night, if he stayed, she would know for sure she'd be safe.

He leaned over and kissed her on her bare shoulder. "Okay, I can do that," he agreed. "But I'll need to leave early in the morning."

"I'll want you to leave early and get back to finding bad guys. You can use the bathroom first."

He slid out of the bed and once again she was gifted to a view of his perfect physique as he picked up his boxers from the floor and then left the room.

She liked Daniel and now she had slept with him, but that certainly didn't mean she wanted any kind of a relationship with him. He was only the first in a string of lovers she might take as she guarded her heart against any entanglements, she thought.

It didn't take him long to return to the room. Clad in his boxers he got back in bed. She got out of the bed, grabbed a nightshirt and a clean pair of panties from a drawer and then went into the bathroom.

For a long moment she stared at her reflection in the mirror that hung on one wall. Her hair was mussed and her lips were slightly swollen. She looked like a woman who had just been completely sated by love-making. And that's exactly what she was.

Daniel had been an amazing lover. At times tender and at other times half wild, he had fulfilled her completely. She'd instinctively known it would be good with him, and it had been better than good. She cleaned up, put on her panties and nightshirt and then returned to the bedroom.

"Don't we need to talk about this?" he asked as she got back into the bed.

"What's there to talk about? We wanted each other…we acted on it and now it's done," she replied lightly. "Don't make it any deeper than it is, Daniel."

He held her gaze for a long moment and then nodded. "Okay."

"Do you want to turn out the light?"

He reached out and shut off the lantern. The only light in the room was now the moonlight that drifted in through the window. He then gathered her into his arms, pulling her close against him in a big spoon fashion.

She snuggled into him, loving the way he felt against her back and how his arm fell around her waist. She felt safe…so safe with him next to her.

The sounds of the swamp drifted in. The water lapped against the legs of the shanty and frogs croaked their night songs. Sleep had been elusive since the night she'd found her mother's body, but now she felt herself drifting off, safe in Daniel's embrace and with the lullaby of the swamp to soothe her.

Chapter Seven

Daniel awakened just around dawn. At some point during the night, he and Angelique had separated from each other. She was now curled up on her side and faced him.

He gazed at her for several long moments, her features barely discernible in the early morning light that seeped into the nearby window.

Even in slumber, the woman was beyond beautiful. Her hair was a cloud of darkness against the lilac-colored pillowcase and her lips were parted slightly as she breathed in and out in the deep rhythm of sleep.

He could have lingered there and gazed at her forever, but he only looked at her for several more long moments, and then he finally slid out of the bed. As quietly as possible he retrieved his clothing from the floor and his gun from the nightstand. Thankfully he managed to get out of the room without waking her.

He dressed quickly, grabbed the note in the plastic bag from the coffee table and then left the shanty. He would have left her a note but he didn't know where to find paper or a pen.

It felt a little boorish after the night they had shared just to sneak off in dawn's early light. He would definitely call her later when she would be up and around.

Shock and awe rode with him as he headed back to his house. The shock came from the fact that she'd pulled him into her bedroom and made love with him. The whole thing had been so unexpected, and he was shocked by how easily he'd capitulated to his own desire for her.

The awe came from the fact that she'd been an amazing lover. She'd been passionate and giving and everything he would want in a partner. But of course, she wasn't his partner. She'd made it very clear that what they had shared really meant nothing to her except for a single night of pleasure.

He wasn't just drawn to her physically. He admired her inner strength and how she was facing the danger that surrounded her. He enjoyed her sense of humor and how easy their conversations were.

He was even more intrigued by her than ever. She'd said she hadn't been with anyone in a long time. So, why now? Why him? He had a feeling that some man had hurt her badly. He had a good idea it wasn't George, so had it been Jason Webber? Or another man altogether?

Had she decided to make love to him to make sure he stayed focused on her cases? Had she really wanted him or had she merely wanted to make sure he remained working hard for her?

These questions continued to whirl through his head when he reached his home. He immediately headed upstairs for a shower and after that he pulled on a clean uniform.

Chief of Police Daniel LeCroix was back on duty. It was time to stop thinking about the night that had passed and the woman who intrigued him. It was time to focus on the two crimes he was desperate to solve.

"Morning, Gus," he greeted the officer at the reception desk.

"Back at you, boss," George replied. "You're here early."

"I woke up a little early this morning and decided to come on in. If there's nothing you need to talk to me about, I'll just be in my office."

"I got nothing except to tell you the coffee is fresh in the break room. I made a new pot about twenty minutes ago, so you'd better get it while it's good."

"Good to know. Thanks, Gus."

Daniel headed down the hallway but before he reached his office, he turned into the break room, where the scent of the rich coffee filled the air.

The room was just big enough to hold two round tables, a counter with a small sink and two vending machines. One offered sodas, juices and water and the other one had everything from nuts to sweet rolls and candy bars.

He walked over to the coffee machine and grabbed one of the foam cups that were stacked up next to it. He filled it with the fresh brew and then continued on to his office.

He sank down in his chair and turned on his computer. As he waited for it to load, he sipped the coffee and tried not to think about the night with Angelique. But it was difficult. Despite his shower, he could imagine he still smelled her scent on his skin. He still remembered the feel of her soft skin beneath his touch.

Once his computer was up and running, he checked his official email and was pleased to see the warrant he needed to search Charles Landry's home. He printed it off and then set it aside to take with him when it got a little bit later.

That would be the next step in the investigation of Mystique's murder, but in the case of the attack on Angelique he had no place to go, no next step to take. He could only hope that with more thought, she'd be able to remember somebody from her past that might have a beef with her.

In the meantime, he'd wait for Luke and Clay to arrive at work, and then they'd execute the search warrant on Landry's place. He hoped they would find something there that would incriminate him in Mystique's murder.

To begin his day, he needed to read the reports from his officers on what had happened in the past twelve hours around town. Mystique's murder and Angelique's attempted murder weren't the only crimes that occurred in the small town.

A shoplifter had been arrested at the convenience store and a break-in had happened at one of the houses just off Main Street. The robbers had gotten away with ninety dollars cash, a computer and a television that would probably show up at the pawnshop. Rob Brighton had been arrested for drunk and disorderly outside the Voodoo Lounge.

It wasn't the first time the thirty-year-old plumber had been arrested for that offense. Rob was a great guy when he was sober, but when he drank too much he got mouthy and picked fights.

Not for the first time, Daniel thanked his lucky stars that the officers on the small police force were all good at their jobs. They could take care of these kinds of things, leaving Daniel to remain focused on the Santori cases.

It was eight o'clock when Daniel, Luke and Clay prepared to go to the Landry home for the search. He also tapped Officers Sam Summers and Roger Teasdale to go with them.

They took off in two cars and headed to the Landry home. Daniel knew Charles Landry had made a small fortune in the stock market. He also owned a textile business that was quite successful. The man was wealthy and yet had needed a love spell cast to help out his romantic life. Unfortunately, the love spell hadn't worked. Had that turned Charles Landry into a killer?

His home was the largest one on Cypress Street. It was a large, two-story painted white with green trim. They pulled up in the double driveway and parked and then got out of the cars.

"I don't expect any trouble, but it's important we be ready for anything," Daniel said before they approached the front door. There was no telling what a murder suspect might do in the name of self-preservation.

"We're ready, Chief," Sam replied. The others murmured their agreement.

"Then let's get to it." Daniel led the small brigade to the front door. He rang the doorbell and heard the musical chimes sound from inside the house.

A moment later the door opened. Charles Landry wasn't a bad-looking guy. His dark brown hair matched the color of his eyes…eyes that widened slightly at the sight of them. He was clad in a pair of brown dress slacks and a brown plaid short-sleeved button-up shirt.

"Gentlemen, what's going on?" he asked with open curiosity.

"We're here to execute a search warrant." Daniel handed him the official piece of paper.

Charles looked it over and then gazed back at Daniel. "You're kidding me, right? This has got to be some kind of a joke."

"It's no joke, Mr. Landry," Daniel replied.

"If you think I killed Mystique Santori because of some stupid love charm, then your investigation is definitely majorly flawed."

"Majorly flawed or not, this is where we are at the moment," Daniel replied curtly. He could feel the man's disdain for them emanating from him. "So, are you going to let us in to do our job?"

"And what if I don't?" Charles asked.

"Then I guess I'll have to arrest you and we'll search your home anyway," Daniel replied.

Charles's nostrils thinned as he opened his door a bit wider. "I certainly don't want to be arrested but I'm warning you now, I have a lot of expensive things in here. If you break anything, I will sue the department."

"Understood," Daniel replied. "We will try to be very careful with your belongings."

"You'd better do better than try." With that, Charles opened the door wide enough for all of them to enter. They walked into a large entry with white marble floors and a small white table with a bronze statue of a woman draped on a chaise lounge.

The living room was large and spotlessly clean. There was a long white sofa and a white chair with glass-topped coffee and end tables. Another bronze statue was on the coffee table, this one of a woman in a rocking chair.

A wet bar was in one corner of the room and a big-screen television hung above a fireplace. "We'll start in here," Daniel said. "Sam and Roger, why don't you start in the wet bar and we'll search the furniture."

"Be careful in the wet bar," Charles said in warning. "I have drink glasses in there that are probably worth half your salaries."

In each room they searched, Charles was there to tell them what everything was worth, and in each of the rooms there were bronze statues of women in various poses and other items that Charles made sure to tell them were expensive.

They thoroughly searched each and every room, and what they didn't find was anything to tie Charles to the murder. No book, no bloody clothes…nothing. It had basically been a whole waste of time.

It was just after eleven when they left the Landry

house. A bitter disappointment filled Daniel as they rode back to the station.

"What about all those women figurines? Creepy, right?" Luke said.

"Totally creepy," Clay agreed.

Was Charles still a suspect? Definitely. He could have Mystique's book in a safe-deposit box or in another city where he had offices.

But once again the case was stuck with no new leads and nowhere to go. When they returned to the station, he went back to his office alone and called Angelique. If nothing else, he wanted to thank her for the delicious dinner she'd made for him the night before.

She answered on the second ring. "Good morning, Daniel."

"Good morning, Angelique," he replied, warmed by the mere sound of her voice.

"I was just calling to thank you for the meal and everything last night," he said. "And to apologize for sneaking out while you were still asleep."

"No problem, I enjoyed the evening very much." Her voice held a bit of heat that stirred him as thoughts of what they had shared flowed through his brain. "And you certainly don't owe me an apology. You had told me you'd be leaving early."

"I was wondering if I could return the favor tonight by taking you to dinner at the café." He hadn't realized he was going to ask her out until the words fell from his lips. Still, it felt right. He'd slept with her, surely a dinner date was in order.

There was a moment of silence, making him wonder if he was completely out of line. “I would love to have dinner with you this evening at the café,” she said, causing a pleasurable anticipation to fill him.

“Great, then how about I meet you at your shanty around six o’clock,” he replied.

“You don’t have to come all the way in here to pick me up. Why don’t I just meet you at the café at six,” she countered.

“Are you sure?”

“Positive,” she replied.

“Okay, then I’ll see you at the café at six this evening.”

They disconnected and Daniel leaned back in his chair. He was ridiculously pleased that she’d agreed to eat with him this evening. It would be another opportunity for him to get to know her better.

What in the hell are you doing, Daniel? Why was he pursuing a social relationship with her? She wasn’t even his type, although he had yet to figure out exactly what his type was.

So far, she had shown none of the controlling issues he had thought she would. She was just passionate about things, and he found that trait very attractive and certainly not off-putting at all.

But what in the serious hell was he doing with her? At this point he really didn’t know.

ANGELIQUE DRESSED WITH care for her evening out with Daniel. She wore a pair of black jeans and a pink-and-black-striped sleeveless blouse. She pulled her freshly washed hair back at the nape of her neck and tied it with a black ribbon and then added a little makeup and black earrings.

When she was finished, she knew she looked casual yet rather hot. The jeans fit her perfectly and she had the blouse unbuttoned just enough to expose her delicate collarbones.

What she didn't understand was why she was going to so much trouble to look good for Daniel. It wasn't like she wanted a relationship with him and she certainly didn't think of tonight as a date.

She just wanted him to find her mother's killer and figure out who wanted her dead, and she was hoping he was the man who would give her those answers.

The only thing different tonight was she'd get a check-in from him over a table at the café instead of here in her shanty. And maybe that was a good thing.

There would be no temptation tonight and he was definitely a temptation. Throughout the day, when she hadn't been racking her brain to figure out who might be after her, she'd been thinking about making love with Daniel.

The whole experience had been beyond breathtaking. Their bodies had fit together as if specifically made for each other. He had taken her to heights of pleasure she'd never been before. Even just thinking about it made her want him all over again.

She hadn't made love with a man since Jason, and those physical unions now seemed weak and mundane when compared to what she'd shared with Daniel the night before.

She hadn't told her sisters about going to dinner tonight. They would somehow try to make it into something it wasn't, and she wasn't in the mood to deal with their silly nonsense. This was just about two people enjoying each other's company and getting information about her mother's murder and nothing more.

At five-thirty she left her shanty. Her purse was slung over her shoulder and the knife was firmly grasped in her hand. She was determined not to be caught unaware again.

Still, as always, she breathed a sigh of relief when she reached the safety of her car. Tomorrow, she had several errands to run. She needed to get more ice for her cooler and gasoline for her generator. Lately she was reluctant to leave the shanty. She felt so vulnerable when she was out and about. But she refused to be a complete shut-in because of some creep.

And who was the creep who apparently wanted her dead? She'd tried to think back in her past, but nothing and nobody came to mind. She didn't go around making enemies. How could she help Daniel catch the attacker when she couldn't think of anyone? And under those circumstances, how could she expect him to come up with the answers?

As she reached Main Street, she shoved all of these thoughts out of her head. She was hungry for both food and any information Daniel had discovered today. She was also looking forward to getting to know the lawman a little better.

When she reached the café, she was lucky to find a parking place close to the front door. She didn't know what kind of a car Daniel drove, but she saw a patrol car parked down the street and suspected it was his.

At precisely six o'clock she walked into the establishment where heavenly scents filled the air. The scents of cooking meats and vegetables mingled with the yeasty fragrance of homemade rolls.

The place was crowded but she saw him immediately. He was seated in a booth and he stood up when he saw her. He was clad in the blue uniform that he wore so well, and he also wore a warm smile that lit up both his features and her insides as she approached.

"Angelique," he said in greeting. "May I just say you look positively terrific tonight."

"Thank you, sir," she replied, ridiculously pleased by the compliment. She slid into the booth seat, and he returned to his seat across from her.

"I hope you're hungry," he said.

"I am. I skipped lunch, knowing I was eating here tonight," she replied. "What about you? Are you hungry?"

"Definitely." He held her gaze for a long moment and then pulled the menus out from where they'd been propped between the salt and pepper shakers. He handed her one and then opened his on the table before him. "You would think with all the times I eat here I would have the entire menu memorized."

"I don't eat here very often, but I have noticed the menu changes with the daily specials." She gazed down at the list of options. "And it looks like today the special is a fried shrimp platter and that sounds good to me." She closed the menu.

"That sounds good to me, too," he replied. He took the menu from her and then placed the two back where they belonged.

By that time Glenda Wright, one of the waitresses, appeared with two glasses of ice water and a bright smile. "Good evening, Chief… Angelique. Have you had a chance to look at the menu or do you need a little more time?"

"We're ready to order," Daniel replied and looked at Angelique to confirm it. She nodded and Daniel ordered two of the shrimp platters. They both ordered iced tea to drink and then Glenda left their booth.

Daniel leaned back and once again held her gaze. "So, you want the bad news first?"

"Sure, why not," she replied. "Let's go ahead and get it over with." A wave of disappointment swept through her even though she hadn't heard the bad news yet.

"We searched Charles Landry's place today and found nothing to tie him to your mother's murder."

"So does that mean he's off the suspect list?" she asked.

"Not at all. It just means we didn't find anything in his house. But if he killed your mother and stole her book, he could have that book anywhere. We're going to learn where he has offices for his business and we'll see that all of those places are searched as well."

"Then what's the good news?" she asked.

He frowned. "I'm afraid there is no good news tonight." He leaned forward and his eyes blazed with a fierce determination. "But we're going to keep digging, Angelique. I swear I won't stop until we have the killer behind bars."

"Thank you, Daniel. I know finding the killer isn't going to be easy, and there will be days when you have nothing to report to me. Now, do you want my bad news first?"

"Might as well get it all out of the way," he replied.

"I thought about who might be my attacker all day long, but I still didn't come up with anyone."

"What's the good news?" he asked.

She released a deep sigh. "There is no good news."

At that moment Glenda reappeared with their iced teas. "Your food should be coming up in just a couple of minutes," she said and left once again.

"I refuse to eat a meal where discouragement is hanging thick in the air," he said. "It gives me indigestion. So, know any good jokes?"

She couldn't help but laugh. "I am not a good joke teller. I always manage to mangle the punch line. Monique is the joke teller in the family. She has perfect timing and could make us all laugh no matter what our mood."

"Were you and your sisters always close?"

"Always. We were…are best friends and there was never a moment when sibling rivalry was an issue. In truth, we had very few friends growing up because we always had each other." She gazed at him curiously. "What about you? Do you have any siblings?" There was so much about him she didn't know.

"No. I had a little brother but he was murdered

along with my mother in a home invasion incident." His eyes appeared to darken with pain.

She gasped in stunned surprise. "Oh my God, Daniel, I'm so very sorry. Did this happen here in Dark Waters?" So he knew intimately the kind of loss that occurred when evil took away a loved one. Still, she couldn't imagine what he'd been through. His mother and his little brother? My God, it was positively horrendous to even think about.

"No, we lived in Baton Rouge, and my father was at work and I was at school when it happened. I was seven years old at the time and my little brother was four. Anyway, afterward my father wanted to get away and so we moved here. I don't even know how he found Dark Waters. But he fell into a deep depression and when I was eighteen years old he wound up taking his own life."

"Oh, Daniel." She reached her hand out to take hold of his. "My God, I had no idea you'd suffered so much."

"It was a long time ago," he replied.

"Even so, it's so horrible. Did they catch the person responsible for your mother and brother's murders?"

"No, they didn't. It's now a cold case that will probably never be solved." He squeezed her hand and she pulled hers back.

"Is that why you went into law enforcement?"

"Yeah. Growing up, all I wanted to do was put all the bad guys away, and I love this little town so law enforcement felt right for me."

"So, you know what it's like," she said softly, giving voice to her earlier thoughts.

"Definitely," he replied. "The only difference between these cases and my mother's and brother's murder is that they became cold cases, and I refuse to allow your mother's murder or the attack on you to go cold."

"I appreciate it," she replied.

Glenda came over and placed their meals in front of them. The shrimp was fried golden brown and it came with a side of seasoned rice, a fresh green salad and a big slab of corn bread.

"We definitely need to lighten the conversation now," Daniel said once Glenda was gone. "Tell me more about growing up with your sisters and with Mystique as your mother."

"My mother wasn't really a hands-on type of parent, although she did homeschool us. She spent our early years teaching us all about the dangers of the swamp. She taught us about every wild animal and what snakes were poisonous and which ones weren't."

She paused to take a sip of her tea and then continued. "By the time I was twelve, Dominique was ten and Monique was nine, we were pretty much running wild in the swamp with a bunch of other swamp kids." She smiled as thoughts of her childhood flittered through her mind. "It was a very carefree and wonderful childhood."

"That's nice," he replied.

She held his gaze for a long moment, her heart hurting for him and what he'd been through. "I wish you would have had that kind of a childhood."

"Thanks. That which doesn't kill us makes us stronger, right? I survived my childhood and it's long in the past. If you don't mind me asking, where was your father in all this?"

"Not around. I don't even know who my father is. Same with Dominique and Monique. Mama refused to tell us. She didn't ever want to discuss the issue. I don't even know if we all had the same father or not."

"Is it possible Pierre could be your father?"

"No. Mama and Pierre didn't start hooking up until I was in my teens. All she told me was that my father didn't want to be a part of my life so at that time I decided it wasn't important for me to know him. Besides, Mama was such a big presence in our life we didn't miss having a father."

"That's good." He picked up his fork and began to eat his salad and she followed suit.

"When you have children, will you want the father to be involved?" he asked between bites.

"If I decide to have children, the answer is a resounding no. I don't intend to ever have any romantic relationships in my life, so I wouldn't want to be bound to a man through a child. I'd raise the child by myself."

He put his fork down and gazed at her in open curiosity. "Why is that?"

"Why is what?" she asked in confusion.

"Why don't you intend to ever have any romantic relationships in your life? Angelique, you're young and quite stunning. You're obviously intelligent and have a great sense of humor. I'm sure there are plenty of men both in the swamp and in town who would be thrilled to be in a relationship with you."

"Men lie and cheat," she replied. "I have no interest in falling in love with another man. I intend to take lovers when I want to, but I will never trust my heart to anyone ever again." She stopped talking as she realized she was giving him too much information about herself.

"Not all men lie and cheat," he protested. "Angelique, tell me what man broke your heart?" he asked softly.

She raised her chin and held his gaze intently. "Nobody," she replied, even though it was a lie. "Don't be mistaken about me, Daniel. I don't have a heart to break. Now let's eat before it all gets cold."

Chapter Eight

The next morning Daniel sat at his desk and thought about the dinner he'd had with Angelique the night before. After their discussion about relationships, their conversation had remained light and casual for the rest of the meal.

Still, she had exposed more of herself than she probably realized. He'd learned that the first man to betray her was the father who didn't want to be a part of her life. She'd said it hadn't mattered, but it had to have hurt a little girl's heart to know her daddy didn't want anything to do with her.

He highly suspected Jason Webber was the man who had broken her heart with lies and cheating. Daniel had gone to school with Jason, and he'd never particularly liked the man to begin with. The fact that he'd broken her heart to the point that it had turned her cynical about all men made Daniel like the man even less.

It was a damned shame. She deserved the love of a good man who would treat her like a queen, a man who would never lie or cheat on her. Unfortunately, she wasn't even giving herself a chance to find that special man. She was closed off to the very idea.

He'd surprised himself by sharing with her the tragedy in his own childhood. It was something he rarely talked about to anyone, and as he'd gained more distance from it, he rarely thought about it. He had very few memories of his mother.

He could still remember the way she smelled like roses and how her hand felt as it stroked across his forehead. He remembered her lips pressed against his cheek as she whispered good-night to him. However, that was pretty much all he had of her.

His memories of his brother were equally as nebulous. He remembered boyish giggles and wrestling together, and that was all he had of a brother named Alan.

With his mother and brother gone, Daniel had to grow up fast, especially when his father had started drinking. His father never got over the murders of his wife and son.

Throughout Daniel's teen years, his father would drink himself stupid and then sit at the kitchen table and weep until he eventually passed out. The murders had absolutely broken his father beyond repair.

So, in reality, like Angelique, he had pretty much grown up without a father. But that was then and this was now, and Daniel rarely allowed himself to wallow in the tragedies of his past.

There had been a time when he'd hoped to have a woman to love and to fill his house with children. He had hoped to build the family he'd never really had, but he just didn't see it happening for him anymore.

That didn't mean he wasn't incredibly drawn to Angelique. He was, and the more he learned about her, the more he wanted to know about her. He wanted to gift her with the solving of her mother's murder and the identity of who had attacked her, but at the moment, much to his frustration, both cases were definitely at a standstill.

When Luke and Clay came in, the three of them sat in the murder room where the whiteboard taunted Daniel with its relative emptiness.

"I still put my money on Pierre," Luke said. "I think it was a crime of passion. I believe that he wanted to get back with Mystique and when she refused, there was a fight."

"The coroner did say the knife used was one like a fishing knife," Clay added.

"Like a fishing knife, but he couldn't say for certain that it was a fishing knife," Daniel reminded them both.

"I'd love to arrest Charles Landry just for being an arrogant ass," Luke said, his distaste for the man obvious in his tone.

"If he mentioned one more time how expensive his things were, I was ready to puke all over those expensive things," Clay replied, making both Luke and Daniel laugh.

"He is a condescending jerk for sure, but what we need to figure out is if he's a cold-blooded killer,"

Daniel said. "It's hard to believe he killed Mystique because the love charm didn't work for him."

"But we all know people murder for crazy reasons," Luke said. "Maybe he didn't want it to get out that he'd gone to Mystique's for a love charm. Maybe he was embarrassed by the whole thing."

A deep frustration ate at Daniel's very soul. "Any more thoughts on who might be after Angelique?"

"I don't have a clue," Luke replied.

"Me, neither," Clay said. "I think the only one who can solve that is Angelique herself."

"And so far that's not happening. She has no clue who might want to hurt or kill her." Daniel took a drink of the cup of coffee before him and then slammed the cup down. "Damn, I'm so frustrated right now."

"Maybe we should pull Pierre in here and sweat him a bit," Luke suggested.

"Maybe you're right," Daniel agreed. "The only time we've spoken with him was during our search warrant." He looked first at Clay and then at Luke. "You two want to bring him in?"

Both officers stood. "It would be our pleasure," Luke replied.

Moments later the two were gone. Daniel kicked himself for not bringing his number one suspect in for more intensive questioning earlier. Pierre would be out of his element here at the police station, and Clay and Luke had a mean bad cop/good cop routine. Maybe it was possible they could sweat him enough to get an admission of guilt from the gator hunter who professed his deep love for Mystique.

It was almost an hour later when the two officers returned with an unenthusiastic Pierre between them. "Let's head to an interview room," Daniel said.

The four of them sat at the small table in a conference room. Pierre was clad in a pair of worn jeans and a stained white T-shirt. He smelled of fish and the swamp waters. Luke sat on one side of him and Clay on the other. Daniel remained standing next to the door.

"I don't know why this is all so necessary. I already told you I didn't have anything to do with Mystique's murder," Pierre said in a surly tone.

"We just wanted to ask you some more questions," Daniel replied. "And it's more comfortable to do it here rather than standing in the heat outside your shanty."

"Well make it fast. I got important things to do," Pierre said.

"Now, exactly where were you at around ten on the night of Mystique's murder?" Luke asked.

Pierre's thick eyebrows drew together. "I told you before I was out in the swamp gator hunting."

"Are you sure you weren't fishing that night?" Luke asked. "I thought you told us when we spoke to you earlier that you were out fishing."

"Hell, I don't know," Pierre replied in obvious irritation. "It was either one thing or another. That's all I do… I fish and I hunt big gators. All I know for sure is I wasn't anywhere near Mystique's place that night."

Luke leaned forward. "There's a lot of gator hunters in the swamp. You mean to tell me nobody saw you out and about on that night?"

"No, nobody saw me. Gator hunting isn't exactly a social affair. I got myself a sweet little honey hole, where there's fish and a big gator that I've been after. Nobody goes to my place. It's a matter of respect."

"Did you catch the gator that night?" Luke asked. Daniel continued standing quietly and watching the emotions that played over Pierre's features. His irritation was obvious not only on his facial features but in the rising tone of his voice as well.

"No, I didn't get him that night or any night since, but sooner or later that big scaly bastard will be mine," Pierre replied.

"So, you don't really have any alibi for the night of Mystique's murder," Luke said flatly.

Pierre's nostrils thinned and a narrow trickle of sweat escaped and ran down the side of his face. Before the three had arrived, Daniel had turned on the heat in the interview room to make it less pleasant.

"I already told you I loved that woman with all my heart and soul and I could never hurt her, let alone kill her," Pierre said. "In all the years Mystique and I were together, I never laid a hand on her."

"But you two were broken up at the time of her murder. Who called things off between the two of you? You or her?" Luke leaned even closer to the man, getting into Pierre's personal space.

"She decided we needed a little time apart," Pierre said after a long pause. "But that was nothing new with us. She'd kick me to the curb for a couple of weeks, and then we'd get back together. It's like we were addicted to each other. We could never stay apart for very long."

"Maybe this time she didn't want to get back together with you. Maybe that night you went to speak with her and she told you she was done with you forever. That made you very angry and a physical altercation ensued and you wound up slitting her throat."

"The hell you say," Pierre replied angrily. He slammed a fist down on the table. "Dammit, that didn't happen." He stared down at the tabletop and drew several deep breaths. It was obvious he was trying to get his temper under control.

For the next thirty minutes or so Luke pressed Pierre hard. "Were you drinking on that night? Is it possible you killed her because you were drunk? Maybe blacked out?"

"Hell no," Pierre replied. "I don't drink when I'm gator hunting. What kind of a damned fool would do that?"

By this time Luke had been questioning the man for almost an hour. "Back off, Luke," Clay said to his partner as part of the bad cop/good cop act. "Pierre, would you like some water or maybe a soda?"

The man released a deep, ragged sigh and swiped the sweat from his face. "A glass of water would be great."

"Let me go get that for you." Clay left the room and returned a moment later with a cold bottle of water. Pierre took it from Clay, cracked it open and drank deeply.

He then offered Clay a grateful smile. "Thanks, man."

The questioning went on for another half an hour

with Luke pressing the man hard, and Clay telling his partner to back off. But despite the aggressive questioning, Pierre stuck to his story—that he hadn't even seen Mystique on the night of her murder.

"That was pretty much a waste of time," Daniel said once Pierre had left the room to go back to the swamp.

"Did you pick up anything on his facial features that might tell you he's lying?" Clay asked.

"Not really, but what I did see was a lot of repressed anger. As far as I'm concerned, he's still our number one suspect," Daniel replied. "But all we have right now is a very weak circumstantial case against him, and I don't believe Jackson will take on the case as it stands right now."

Jackson Scott was the district attorney. Generally, he was a good friend of law enforcement, but he ruled strictly by the book, and there just wasn't enough here for him to want to take on the case.

"At least we now have his fingerprints, thanks to the bottle of water we gave him," Luke said.

"Yeah, but so far we have nothing to compare them to," Clay replied.

"That could change once we get things back from the lab," Luke said.

"Maybe we need to go back to the swamp and find out who Pierre runs with. He might not drink when he's gator hunting, but maybe he has some friends he drinks with when he's not hunting. Perhaps he told one of his buddies about the murder," Daniel said thoughtfully.

"Then why hasn't anyone come forward?" Clay asked.

"You know those gator hunters hang tight with each other, and they have a general distrust of law enforcement," Daniel said. "Still, I think it's best if we spend the afternoon talking to as many of the gator hunters as we can find."

Daniel looked at his watch. "Why don't we break for lunch now and meet back here at one o'clock." It was now a quarter after twelve. "At that time, we'll head back into the swamp and hopefully find someone who Pierre trusted with all his secrets."

"Sounds like a good plan. I'm heading to The Burger Joint. Do you want me to pick you up something?" Clay asked.

"Yeah, just get me the usual," Daniel replied. The usual was a double cheeseburger and fries.

The two men left the room and Daniel headed to his office. It was only noon and he was already tired. With a plan to continue his investigation into Pierre set, he now thought about how he could continue moving forward in Angelique's case.

The fact that she couldn't think of anyone she'd had words with in the past spoke highly of her pleasant personality. But there had to be somebody she had ticked off.

Marianne Lutgen. Was it possible the swamp woman had built up a deep resentment…a hatred for Angelique? He definitely needed to have a little chat with her. According to Angelique, Marianne might have also had a deep resentment toward Mystique. Definitely somebody who needed to be questioned.

The men returned with their lunches, and Daniel told them about his plan to find Marianne in the swamp and interview her. He wanted his two top officers to be with him as he never knew what he might encounter in the thick vegetation and wildness of the swamp.

"We go from a stinky gator hunter to a cute gal who likes to party." Luke shook his head and grinned. "Never a dull moment in Dark Waters."

They finished eating and were about to leave the office when Daniel's phone rang. It was Jacque LeBlanc, the gator hunter who lived in the very depths of the swamp.

"Ranger Chauvin," Jacque said.

"What about him?" Daniel asked.

"He's always been a strange dude, but he's definitely being more secretive and stranger lately. While out in the swamp I've heard him mumbling to himself, and several times in the last couple of days I've heard him mention Mystique and Angelique's names. His shanty is just to the north of mine."

"Thanks," Daniel said. "I appreciate the tip." When he hung up the phone, a new bolt of adrenaline rushed through him. "A new suspect…let's head out."

Once they were all three in the car, Daniel explained what Jacque had said. "You two know anything about this Ranger guy?" Daniel asked.

"I've seen him around town. From what I know of him, he's not a very friendly guy," Luke said.

"Doesn't he hang out around the hardware store?" Clay asked.

"That's where I usually see him," Luke replied.

"What in the hell does he have to do with Mystique and Angelique," Daniel asked.

"Hopefully, we're going to find out," Luke replied.

They rode in silence to the swamp entrance. A new hope swept through Daniel as he considered another suspect. When they reached the swamp, they walked for about a half an hour into the thick vegetation. When they were almost to Jacque's place, they began to look for a shanty to the north of his.

"This looks like the place," Daniel said as they came upon a small shanty not too far from Jacque's. The boards of the structure were a weathered gray and the front window sported dirty curtains, but no glass.

As they approached, Daniel caught a whiff of the scent of acetone and rotten eggs and cat pee. Apparently, Ranger had a meth lab either inside his shanty or someplace nearby.

Out of an abundance of caution, Daniel pulled his revolver, and Luke and Clay did the same. "Ranger Chauvin," Daniel yelled when they reached the bottom of the porch stairs.

There was no response. "Ranger, it's the police department…come on out," Daniel yelled loudly.

The door flew open and a tall, lanky man stepped out. He had on a pair of jeans and a dirty blue T-shirt, and it appeared he not only cooked the illegal drug, but also indulged in it as well. His thin face had the typical meth sores that he obviously picked.

"What's up? What's up?" he asked, his features twitching as he danced back and forth from foot to foot. "What do you want? What are you all doing here?"

"Ranger, we have a few questions to ask you," Daniel said.

"I got answers," Ranger replied. "I got plenty of answers, so ask away."

"How well did you know Mystique Santori?"

Ranger's eyes opened wide. "You mean the witch lady? It's a good thing somebody slit her throat and killed her so she couldn't say anymore wicked curses."

"Did she put a wicked curse on you, Ranger?"

"She might have," the man replied as his dark eyes narrowed. He reached up a hand and worried one of the sores on his cheek. "I think she did. Yup, I'm almost positive she did."

"Why would she do such a thing to you?" Daniel asked. He put his gun back in the holster as he felt no physical threat with the man.

A smile slowly curved his lips. "'Cause I told her I wanted her daughter."

"Which daughter?" Daniel asked.

"Angelique. That Angelique is mighty fine, and I intend to have her as my own one day very soon. I plan to marry that woman."

"What did Mystique say to you when you told her that?" Daniel asked. A new tension swept through him. Was it possible he was looking at the man who had killed Mystique and attacked Angelique? Was he the person who had left that note on the door for Angelique to find?

Ranger's smile turned into a deep frown. "She laughed at me. The bitch told me I would never be good enough for her daughter, and that's when I think she cursed me 'cause after that she haunted me in my dreams…very bad dreams."

"I'm sure all that made you very angry," Daniel said.

"Oh, it did. For sure it did." He dropped his hand back to his side.

"Were you angry enough to slice her throat, Ranger?" Daniel asked.

"Whoa." Ranger took a step backward. "I had nothing to do with that. You can't pin that on me because I didn't kill anyone, especially the witch lady. I was scared of her."

"What about Angelique? Did you break into her shanty in an effort to hurt her or maybe kidnap her?" Daniel asked.

"Hell no." The man was beginning to get quite agitated. He continued to dance from foot to foot, and his whole body twitched.

"I had nothing to do with that," he said. "I would never attack Angelique or try to hurt her. She's like a queen…a goddess on earth. When I'm ready, I intend to court her like a real gentleman. Why are you after me anyway? I catch fish and gators—that's all I do."

"That's not quite true," Daniel said. "I can smell what else you do, Ranger," Daniel said.

Ranger narrowed his eyes once again. "I don't know

what you're talking about." His body tensed up as he glared at Daniel.

"Why don't you let us inside and show us around your shanty?" Daniel said.

"I don't got to let you in," Ranger countered as his body tensed up even more.

"Don't make things difficult on yourself, Ranger. I can have a search warrant for your shanty in my hand within the next half an hour or so. Just let us in now and if you aren't doing anything wrong, then we'll get out of your face."

Ranger stared at him for a long moment, and then he suddenly lunged off the porch and headed into the woods. "Stop," Daniel cried.

"Ranger, halt or I'll tase you," Luke yelled.

The three men gave chase as Ranger raced just ahead of them. Bushes scratched and ripped at Daniel's arms and more than once a tuber threatened to trip him up.

He didn't see the gun. He didn't see it until Ranger stopped, pulled it out of the back of his jeans and fired.

BY NINE O'CLOCK that evening Angelique assumed Daniel wasn't coming. It would have been nice if he'd called to let her know that, but he hadn't.

She decided to go ahead and change into her new, forest-green nightgown. She'd thrown away the nightwear that she'd had on when she'd been attacked and had decided today that it was time for a new one. She'd made a quick stop into All That Jazz, and now it was time to change into what she'd bought.

She'd spent much of the afternoon running errands. Along with the nightgown and matching robe, she'd picked up the gasoline for her generator and a new block of ice for her cooler.

She'd also stopped in the grocery store and had picked up a few more things. She now had everything she needed to stay in her shanty for about a week without needing to go out for anything.

It had been gloomy all afternoon, and she had just gotten home from running her errands when the skies opened up and it began to rain. Even now as she got ready for bed, a steady rain beat down on the roof. It was rhythmic and soothing.

Sleep wasn't quite ready to take her yet, so she grabbed the book she'd been working on and curled up on the sofa. She began to read back over what she'd already written.

It contained not only the recipes for some of the remedies, but also where in the swamp to find the necessary ingredients. She hadn't been reading very long when she heard the creak of the boards on her bridge. Somebody was coming.

She got up from her sofa and grabbed the knife that she always kept near her. She assumed it was Daniel, but she certainly wasn't taking any chances.

A knock fell on the door. "Angelique, it's me," his familiar voice called out.

She set the knife down on the end table and then hurried to open the door. "Hurry, get in out of the rain." She grabbed his hand and pulled him over the threshold.

"Just let me go get my robe." She dropped his hand and hurried into her bedroom to grab the matching robe that went with the nightgown.

Even though she had already slept with him, that didn't mean she felt comfortable enough to sit around half naked with him. She pulled the silky robe around her and tied it at her waist then stopped in the bathroom where she grabbed a clean towel from a shelf. She then returned to the living room, where he was seated on the sofa.

"Here, take this and dry yourself off," she said and handed him the towel. She gasped in stunned surprise as she got her first real look at him. He wore jeans and a navy-blue T-shirt, but what really caught her eye and made her gasp was the large bandage on his upper arm.

"Oh, Daniel, what happened?" She sank down on the sofa next to him.

"It's a gunshot wound, but I'll get to that," he replied. He took a moment and ran the towel over his wet hair and then placed the towel next to him on the sofa and gazed at her.

"We started the morning by pulling in Pierre for a deeper, more intense interrogation. We were hoping if he was our man, we could get him to crack and confess."

"And he shot you?" she asked, bewildered by how that could have happened. "Oh, Daniel, are you all right?" She couldn't believe he'd been shot.

"No, it wasn't him and I'm fine. Anyway, Pierre didn't confess. After that we had the intention to speak with Marianne Lutgen…"

"And she shot you?" Angelique gasped again in stunned surprise.

He laughed. "Woman, would you be patient. I'll get to who shot me in a minute. Anyway, before we could leave the station to find Marianne, we got a tip that we needed to look at Ranger Chauvin. Do you know him?"

She frowned. "Yeah, I know him only very casually. I've heard whispers that if you want some meth or other drugs, Ranger is the man to see."

He nodded. "As soon as we approached his cabin, we could smell the scent of meth cooking. But what was really surprising is apparently Ranger has a real thing for you."

"A thing for me?" Once again, she stared at him in shock. "What does that even mean?"

"Apparently, he spoke to your mother about his wild desire for you and his intentions to date you and make you his own. She made him very angry by laughing in his face and telling him he wasn't good enough for you."

"I… I'm stunned. I didn't know anything about this," she replied. "Mama never mentioned it to me."

"He believes she then put a spell on him that made her appear in nightmares he suffered," Daniel continued.

"So, he had reason to want my mother dead."

"That's what we believe. Unfortunately, before we could really dig into that, I made the mistake of mentioning the meth issue," he said.

He told her about Ranger jumping from his porch

and then running away and the chase that ensued. "None of us knew he was armed." Daniel frowned. "It was our mistake for not checking him when we first approached. Thank God, the bullet he fired only grazed my arm."

She grabbed hold of his hand and held it tightly. "You could have been killed."

His jaw muscles tightened. "Yeah. Thank God, Ranger was hyped up enough on his meth so he couldn't shoot straight, otherwise it could have been much worse. Anyway, that's my investigation report for the night."

"To heck with the investigation. I don't care about that right now. I just need to know that you're going to be okay," she replied worriedly. "What did the doctor say?"

"Why, Miss Santori, if you keep talking to me so sweet, I might think you actually care about me," he said, a teasing blue sparkle in the depths of his eyes.

"Don't flatter yourself," she replied and dropped his hand.

He laughed once again, as if amused by her perverseness.

"Actually, I was lucky that I was just grazed. According to the doctor, all I have to do is keep antibiotic cream on it and keep it covered for a few days," he said, more serious now. "Sound familiar?"

She held his gaze for several long moments. Oh, he had such beautiful eyes. It would be so easy to fall into the blue depths. "I'm just glad you're okay. I have to admit, Daniel, I've grown quite fond of you."

"I could say the same about you," he replied softly.

As their gazes remained locked, she wanted to fall into his arms once again. She wanted to take him by the hand and lead him to her bedroom for another bout of lovemaking, but she was oddly afraid of the new feelings for him that swept through her.

"Then is Ranger now your top suspect?" she asked, wanting to focus on what was less threatening and the reason he was here.

"No, my money is still on Pierre. Whoever killed your mother managed to get in and get out without leaving anything behind as evidence. I'm not sure Ranger could achieve that, given his drug use. In any case, Ranger is now in custody so we'll have full access to question him once he's clear minded and as soon as he gets out of the hospital."

"The hospital?"

He grinned. "Yeah, once he shot me, Luke shot him in the lower leg. At least we managed to take down a meth lab, and Ranger will be facing a number of serious charges."

"That's a good thing," she replied.

"Tell me about your relationship with Jason Webber."

She stared at him in surprise as the question seemed to come out of thin air. "Why would you want to know about that? Is this really a part of your investigation?"

"Angelique, I need to go back in your past and figure out who might have a beef with you. The one part of your life we haven't discussed so far is your relationship with Jason. So, how long did the two of you date?"

This was the very last thing she'd expected to be talking about tonight, and she found herself reluctant to go back to that painful part of her past.

She released a deep sigh. "We dated for just a little bit over a year."

"And who broke up with whom?" He gazed at her with open curiosity."

She hated the old feelings the conversation evoked inside her. She hated to even think about the man who had lied to her for months. "I broke up with him. I found out he had been cheating on me all throughout our relationship, and once I learned that, I immediately tossed him to the curb."

"How did he react when you broke up with him?" Daniel asked.

"He was upset and of course told me my information was wrong and he wasn't cheating on me, but I was certain of my facts because I had spoken to the woman he was cheating on me with. He called me a couple of times after that, but I told him there was no going back and that I never wanted to see him again."

"Do you believe he was angry with you?" Daniel leaned a little closer, bringing with him the scent of his attractive cologne.

"Certainly he wasn't angry enough to attack me in the middle of the night with a knife."

"How did he get along with your mother?"

"Actually, very well. Mama liked him because she could see how happy he made me. Of course, when she found out he was a liar and a cheater, she was very angry with him. But Daniel, this was so long ago, and

Jason has dated dozens of women since then. I can't imagine how any of that has anything to do with the crimes you are now investigating."

"He broke your heart," he replied as he gazed at her softly.

She flushed and broke eye contact with him. She focused on the wall just over his shoulder. "He taught me all I need to know about men, so in the end I believe he did me a big favor."

"Angelique, not all men lie and cheat," he countered.

She released another deep sigh and looked at him once again. "We've had this discussion before, Daniel, and you aren't going to change my mind. I will never again fully trust another man with my heart." She frowned, wanting to change the topic. "Besides, you haven't told me anything about your past relationships."

"There isn't a lot to tell," he replied. "The most serious relationship I had was a little over two years ago when I started dating Allison Gregory. Do you know her?"

She frowned thoughtfully and then slowly shook her head. "No, I don't believe so."

"She was a receptionist in one of the dental offices in town. Anyway, we started dating, and after three months it was decided she'd move in with me. Almost from the very beginning after that there were problems."

"Problems like what?" she asked curiously.

"Well, like the first thing she did was quit her job. I didn't really have a problem with it because I made enough in my job to support us. But what I did have a problem with was then her job became all about controlling me."

She was finding this all fascinating and hoped he'd continue to share with her about his failed relationship. "I have a nice bottle of brandy in the kitchen. Would you like to have a glass with me?"

"Sure," he agreed. "That sounds good. A little alcohol is surely warranted on a night when I got shot."

She got up from the sofa. "Sit tight and I'll be right back." It was definitely an evening of surprises. First the fact that he'd been shot, which explained why he didn't stop by with his report earlier, and now the glimpses into his past. It didn't take her long to pour the fragrant amber liquid into two glasses and carry them back to the living room.

"Thanks," he said as he took one from her. She sank back down on the sofa next to him.

"So, tell me more about this controlling relationship you found yourself in," she said.

He stared down at the liquid in his glass for a long moment and then took a sip. "Hmm, very nice." He leaned back and stared thoughtfully at a place just over her head as a frown cut across his forehead.

"It started small. I thought it was cute when she bought me a half a dozen new shirts that weren't really my style but rather what she liked. However, I didn't think it was so cute when she threw all my other shirts away."

"Oh, you don't mess with a man's fashion," she replied.

He looked at her again and smiled. "She not only messed with my fashion, she stopped allowing me to eat meat and she'd show up at my work to check what I'd ordered for lunch. She was slowly consuming my life with her control issues, and after three months together, I'd finally had enough. So, I asked her to leave my house and my life."

She took a sip of the brandy and then studied his features for a long moment. "Did it all break your heart?" she finally asked.

"In a way. I was certainly disappointed, but by the time I asked her to leave, I was more than ready to see her go." He gazed at her intently. "Now, I could draw a conclusion from my experience with her that all women are controlling, just like you have drawn a conclusion from your experience with Jason that all men are liars and cheats."

She finished the last sip of her brandy. "Daniel, why does it matter so much to you what I believe about men? Why do you even care if I never have a romantic relationship in my life again? Why do you care if I'm never in love again?" she asked.

"It just bothers me, that's all." He stood. "And now it's late and I need to head home. Needless to say, it's been a very long day."

She got up as well and walked with him to the front door. He turned back to face her. "Thanks for the brandy," he said and leaned closer to her.

"You're welcome and thank you for the information you bring to me every night." Was it normal that every time he stood so near to her, her heart quickened?

"Angelique, you asked me why it matters to me whether you ever find love again." His eyes held an indistinguishable light she couldn't read.

He reached out and gently moved a strand of her hair behind her ear. "Let me tell you what I think. I think you're a woman who needs to be loved deeply and I'm not talking about an occasional roll in the hay. I want a man for you who will cherish the very ground you walk on and share every dream you have. And now I'll just say good night and I'll see you tomorrow." Before she could respond, he kissed her lightly on the forehead, turned on his heels and walked off.

Chapter Nine

Another week passed of interviews that gave up nothing, of leads that went nowhere and both cases stalling to the point of sheer madness.

The only things not stalling were his growing feelings for Angelique. Each day he was eager to cross the bridge to her shanty and every night he was reluctant to leave it.

The woman he had first met to get her out of his investigations, the one he'd believed was a complete control freak, was nothing like the Angelique he'd come to know.

What he'd come to know about her was that she was kind and warm and giving in nature. She was bright and funny and they shared the same sense of humor.

Since the night he had spoken to her so candidly about the kind of love he wanted her to find, something in their relationship had subtly changed.

Their conversations since then had been deeper… more intimate and he was enjoying getting to know all the facets of her personality. He had also found himself sharing with her more of himself than he thought he'd ever shared with a woman before.

He'd talked to her more about his childhood and life with his father, while she shared bits and pieces of her relationship with Jason. They'd talked about failed dreams and new ones and the murders that had forever changed both of their lives.

It worried him. He was falling for her, and yet he saw no real indication that she felt the same about him. The sexual tension was still off the charts between them, but they hadn't made love again.

Had she pulled him into her bedroom the first time because she'd desired Daniel the man or because she wanted to make sure Daniel the lawman remained committed to solving the cases?

Was she still being so friendly to him in the evenings because she enjoyed their time together? Or did she have the ulterior motivation of keeping him producing on the cases?

He didn't like to think about her like that, but he just wasn't sure what to believe where she was concerned. She was like no other woman he had ever known. All he knew for sure was he was getting in way too deep with her and he wasn't sure what to do about it.

During the past week they had interviewed Marianne Lutgen and she had confessed to them that she didn't particularly like Angelique. She found Angelique snooty in not wanting to join in the parties Marianne threw. It was ironic that a party was her alibi for both the night of Mystique's murder and Angelique's attack.

Tonight, he'd asked Angelique if she'd like to have dinner at his house. He thought a change of scenery might be good for them both. The shanty was full of her scent and made it difficult for him to focus. It held the memories of their intimacy, also making it difficult for him to think straight.

Besides, tonight he intended to tell her that the nightly check-ins were coming to an end. They were beginning to feel too much like pleasure rather than work. Things were moving so slowly in the cases he figured once-a-week check-ins would be more appropriate.

It would definitely be mentally healthy for him to pull back on seeing her so often. He needed to protect himself from his growing feelings for her.

It was just before five on another unproductive day when he, Clay and Luke sat in his office. "I don't see anything on tap for tomorrow as far as the investigations go," Daniel said dispiritedly.

"We've explored every avenue that's come up so far. I still believe eventually Pierre is going to break and confess to somebody that he killed Mystique, and hopefully when he does talk, the person he talks to will come straight to us," Luke said. "I still believe that murder was a crime of passion."

"I agree," Clay added. "The attack on Angelique is far more complicated, and I'm afraid the only way we might get more clues about it is if the attacker comes for her again."

Daniel's muscles tensed at the very thought. The idea of another attack on her scared him to death. "Too bad there were no fingerprints on the note the attacker left for her."

"That would have made it all too easy," Luke replied.

"Something will give," Clay said optimistically. "Somebody will talk or a new suspect will show himself. One way or another, we're going to get both Mystique's killer and Angelique's attacker behind bars."

"On that optimistic note, I'm heading home," Daniel said and rose from his desk. The other men got up and together they all left the office. "I'll see you two in the morning."

"Good night, boss," Luke said.

"See you in the morning," Clay added.

Moments later, Daniel was in his car and headed home. Thankfully, before leaving for work that morning he'd prepared everything he could for the evening meal.

The table was set for two. The potatoes were washed, wrapped in aluminum foil and ready to pop into the oven. Two nice rib eye steaks were marinating in the fridge, and he'd chopped up cucumbers, celery and carrots to add to a salad.

Once home, he turned on the oven, popped the potatoes in and then went upstairs for a quick shower. He dressed in a pair of jeans and a blue-and-gray T-shirt.

Angelique had insisted she'd come to him, although he would have preferred that he pick her up and take her home at the end of the evening. But she'd insisted she could drive herself and there was no need for him to drive into the swamp to get her.

As he waited for her to arrive, he began to set things on the table. The salt and pepper shakers sat next to a small carton of butter and a bowl of sour cream for the baked potatoes. He then began putting together the salad. He'd just finished and set it in the center of the table when his doorbell rang, announcing her arrival.

As always when he was about to see her, a sweet anticipation soared through him. Tonight was no different. She looked lovely, clad in a pair of black jeans that hugged her long, slender legs and a crisp white sleeveless blouse. Her hair was in a high pony with a white-and-black polka-dot bow. She looked positively stunning. She looked classy and sexy at the same time.

"Welcome to my home," he said as he stepped aside so she could come in the front door.

"Thank you," she replied.

"Did you have any trouble finding it?"

"Not at all. Your directions brought me right to you with no problem," she replied.

"Good. Come on into the kitchen and sit." He led her through the living room and into the kitchen, where he gestured for her to sit at the table.

"You have a lovely home," she observed.

"Thanks, I like it here, although there are times I think about selling it."

"Why?"

"It's a lot of house for a single guy," he replied. "Are you hungry?"

"Of course. You said to bring my appetite, so I did," she replied with one of her endearing grins. "Now, what can I do to help?"

"Absolutely nothing. The potatoes are going to take another twenty minutes or so, and then I'm putting the steaks outside on the grill and they will only take about fifteen minutes. By the way, how do you like your steak?"

"Medium rare."

"Ah good, that makes it easy for the cook. That's the way I like mine, too." He sat down in the chair facing her. "So, how was your day?"

"It was good…quiet. Dominique came over for lunch, and then after she left, I worked until it was time to get ready to come here. How was your day?"

He frowned. "Unfortunately, I have nothing to report tonight. I'm not going to lie, the cases have both stalled out."

"What, exactly, does that mean?"

"It means until somebody talks or your attacker comes at you again, we have nothing new to investigate." He leaned forward. "I swear, Angelique, if I could, I would have your mother's murderer behind bars right now. I would definitely have the person who came after you behind bars as well."

She reached out and covered one of his hands with hers. "It's okay, Daniel. I know you're doing everything you can to find the bad guys."

"I just wish it was enough. I'm supposed to get the bad guys in jail. That's my job, and right now I feel like I'm failing at it miserably."

"You'll get the bad guys," she replied. "We all just need to be a little patient. I knew solving Mama's murder was going to be difficult, and as far as the attack on me, I haven't been able to give you anything to go on." She pulled her hand back from his.

He smiled at her for a long moment. "You are absolutely nothing like what I initially thought you were going to be," he said.

She released a small laugh. "What's that supposed to mean?"

He leaned back in his chair. "When I first met you, I thought you were going to be a controlling witch. I figured you'd ride me hard and expect unreasonable progress in a complicated murder case. Instead, you've been quite the opposite. You've been very patient and understanding, and you'll never know how much I appreciate it."

"And when I first met you, I thought you were going to be a real hard-ass jerk who would reluctantly dole out information to me as you saw fit. Funny how first impressions aren't always the right ones."

"By the way, you look quite pretty tonight."

She smiled in obvious pleasure. "Why, thank you, kind sir. How is your arm doing?"

"Good, it's pretty much healed up. We've both survived our war wounds."

She laughed, the musical sound so pleasant to his ears. "And hopefully we won't get any more."

"Amen to that," he replied. "And, on that note, I'm going to head outside and get the steaks on." He got up from the table. "You just sit tight right here. Can I get you something to drink before I go out?"

"No thanks, I'm fine."

If it wasn't so hot outside, he would have set the table on his patio so they could eat out there, but the night was sultry and the air was thick, making it unpleasant to be outside. It was only going to get worse as the summer months went on. *Thank goodness for air-conditioning*, he thought.

The gas grill fired right up and within minutes he had the steaks cooking. It had been the perfect time for him to escape the kitchen and Angelique. Tonight, he was feeling particularly vulnerable to his own feelings where she was concerned.

He was in love with her. The sudden realization struck him like a thunderbolt out of the sky. He didn't know exactly when it had happened. He couldn't pick out one specific moment when he'd fallen for her. And in any case, it didn't matter. What did matter was he was hopelessly, crazy in love with her and he wasn't sure what to do about it.

Do nothing, he told himself. No good could come from him sharing his feelings for her. Besides, just because he was in love with her, that didn't mean she felt the same way about him. He might just be the first in a long string of lovers she'd take. The very idea of her casually taking lovers hurt his heart. She deserved so much more than that.

By the time the steaks were cooked, he had his emotions back under control. He carried the steaks inside, where he plated them along with the baked potatoes.

"This looks yummy," she said as he set her plate before her.

"I hope it tastes yummy," he replied as he sank down across from her. "Do you need any steak sauce?"

"Heavens no, why would I want to mess with the taste of the steak?"

He laughed. "I'll ask you about the steak sauce again once you've taken a bite. You might need to mess with the taste of the steak."

As they ate, they talked about the Fourth of July celebration that had just passed. "It was a lot of fun," she said. "It's always fun when a carnival comes to town."

"We're lucky to get the carnival since we're such a small town," he replied.

He'd been on duty that day, but he'd seen the three Santori women together, enjoying themselves. "Did you try to win a stuffed animal at any of the booths?"

"We shot guns and picked up floating ducks and played ring toss, but none of the three of us won anything."

"Did you get a ride on the Ferris wheel?" he asked.

"Not me," she said and laughed. "Dominique and Monique rode it but I don't like heights."

"Really? I would have guessed there was nothing you were afraid of," he replied. *Except falling in love again*, he thought.

"There aren't many things I'm afraid of, but heights is definitely one of them. What about you? Do you have any fears like that?" Her beautiful eyes gazed at him curiously.

"I have a secret fear of dancing deer in pink bikinis," he replied somberly.

Her lips twitched with a suppressed grin. "Are you afraid of normal deer?"

"No, they're just fine. It's the ones that dance and wear the bikinis that frighten me."

She laughed. "You are a real goof," she said.

"I know," he replied with a wide grin.

"I like that about you." She took several bites of her potato.

Her words warmed his heart. Damn, he had it bad for her and that wasn't necessarily good. It made it all that much more important that he stop spending time with her every night.

"I INSIST ON helping with the cleanup," she said once they were finished eating.

"And I insist you don't," he countered. "It will just take me a couple of minutes to get things cleared away, and then we can sit and chat in the living room."

She watched him as he carried the dirty dishes to the sink, rinsed them and then put them into the dishwasher. "That's one thing I wish I could have in my shanty," she said.

"A dishwasher? I would think you'd rather have a refrigerator than a dishwasher," he replied.

"It's a toss-up."

He retrieved the butter and sour cream from the table and put them into the refrigerator. "Have you ever thought about moving to town? Maybe when you open that storefront you want?"

"I've considered it. Don't get me wrong, I love the swamp and I will always think of it as home, but once I have the store, it will be a long trek back and forth every day from the shanty. I've been considering maybe renting a small apartment."

"Still keeping the shanty?" he asked.

"Dominique would probably move into it. Her place is really small, and she's mentioned that if I move to town, then she'd move into my shanty."

"It would be quite a change for you," he observed.

"Yeah, I could have a refrigerator and a dishwasher," she replied with a grin.

By that time the kitchen was clean. "Why don't we head into the living room? Would you like an after-dinner drink? I have some wine, if you'd like a glass. I should have offered you some before dinner."

She got up from the table. "No, thank you on the wine. I'm good." She didn't want anything that might dizzy her senses. They were already dizzied enough by his handsome presence.

There was just something about Daniel that made her feel young and innocent again. He brought forth a girlish delight when his gaze lingered on her for a touch too long or when his smile was so open and warm.

"Thank you for the meal," she said as she sat on the dark brown sofa. His living room was a pleasant space, although it didn't give away much as to the man who lived here. There was nothing personal in the room at all. "It was all really delicious," she added.

"Grilling steaks is the one kind of cooking I can do right," he replied as he sank down next to her. "So, what's on your agenda for tomorrow?" he asked.

"I'm actually meeting with the Realtor, Julia Moore, and she's going to show me some of the available storefronts in town."

An edge of excitement surged inside her. It was finally coming to fruition. She believed she'd saved an adequate amount of money to commit to making the move into owning a store.

"Wow…so it's really happening for you," he said, his eyes lighting up.

"A little faster than I'd expected," she admitted. "But I'm more than ready for it."

"If you see a place that you like tomorrow, then what happens?" he asked.

"Then I sign a contract. It will probably take me another month or two to get the store interior the way I want it—I've seen in it my dreams a million times—and then it will take me some time to gather my inventory. I…" She broke off, aware that she was rambling. "Sorry…needless to say I'm getting excited about it all."

"As you should be. Please, don't apologize. I love your passion," he replied, his gaze warm on her.

"I know it sounds rather silly, but I feel like this is a way to keep my mother's legacy alive. No matter what people thought about her, she was a healer first, and that's what I want people to remember about her."

"I'm sure the shop is going to be very successful," he replied. "However, there's one thing I need you to remember whenever you're out running around."

His eyes appeared to darken and simmer with concern. "You don't have to tell me, Daniel," she said. "I never forget that somebody is after me, and I'm on guard for another attack every time I leave the shanty."

"Dammit," he said. "I hate this for you, and I hate

the fact that we can't get this person identified and behind bars."

"Eventually whoever it is will be caught," she said with a confidence she didn't quite feel. "Besides, nothing has happened since the note was left on my door. Maybe the person has moved on and is no longer after me."

"That's dangerous thinking," he warned her. "You can't think that way because it might make you careless with your safety."

"I know." She released a deep sigh.

For the next hour or so they talked about more pleasant things. She told him more about her vision for the shop, and he shared with her funny stories of his police work. She then shared funny stories about growing up with her sisters.

It was a pleasant time and she thoroughly enjoyed their conversation. She gazed out the window, where twilight shadows had moved in.

"I think it's probably time for me to head home."

"Before you go, there's one more thing I want to talk to you about," he said.

"What's that?" He suddenly looked so serious, and a wave of apprehension shot off inside her.

"Since the cases have stalled, there's really no reason for me to continue with the nightly check-ins. I think it's time I change them to once a week or so."

She wanted to protest, but she knew he was probably right. He'd been very accommodating to do the nightly check-ins with her for as long as he had. It would be selfish of her to demand he continue them.

"I understand," she replied. "Daniel, I appreciate everything you've done for me so far."

"So, how about we set it up that I'll check in with you every Saturday night," he suggested.

"Okay, that works for me," she agreed, even though she would miss seeing him every night. "And now, if that's it, I'm going to get out of your hair and head home." She got up from the sofa and he rose as well.

"Thank you again, Daniel, for the lovely dinner." She walked to the front door and then turned to face him.

His gaze on her was so warm. There had been a simmer going on between them all evening. If he asked her to stay the night, she would. There was really nothing more she'd rather do than finish the night being held in his arms.

But he didn't ask and so she didn't stay. Fifteen minutes later she was in her car and headed home. It was probably a good thing they were only going to see each other once a week from here on out.

Her feelings for him had become more complicated. She enjoyed spending her evenings with him. She liked everything about him. In fact, if she allowed it, she might be falling in love with him. And that scared her.

It was definitely time to put the brakes on. She didn't want a relationship with him, so there was no point in spending any more extra time with Daniel. She wanted updates on the investigations from him and nothing more.

She just wasn't sure why these thoughts caused a shaft of pain to sear through her.

The next week the days flew by. She found the storefront she wanted and signed a year-long contract. Thankfully the interior was already set up with display shelves and counters.

She arranged for Matt Green, the local contractor and handyman, to paint the interior a light seafoam green. Then she talked to Larry Carlson, who owned a sign company, about what she wanted as a sign outside the store.

When she wasn't working at her regular job, she surfed the internet, looking for items she could sell that would make good companions to her homemade remedies.

As fun and exciting as the days were, in contrast the evenings dragged on long and lonely. She missed Daniel. She missed their long conversations and their shared laughter. She missed the scent of him and his very presence.

She hadn't realized just how much she'd enjoyed having his company each night until it was gone. It irritated her that she'd allowed him to get so close, that she'd allowed him to creep so deeply into her heart.

Did he miss her? Or had he been relieved that he no longer had to spend each evening with her? And why did she care? It wasn't like they had a real relationship.

On Friday afternoon, she stood outside her storefront and watched as Larry and his assistant hung the new sign over the front door.

Mystique's Magic. The letters were in bright purple against a seafoam green. The sign was quite eye-catching. She'd decided to make the store an homage to her mother.

"Angelique."

She whirled around at the sound of the familiar voice. "Hi, George," she said.

George approached her with a wide grin. He pointed to the sign. "So, you're finally doing it," he said.

"I am," she agreed with a smile of her own. In the brief time she had dated George, she had spoken to him about her desire to open a storefront.

"Your mother would be so very proud of you," he replied.

"Thanks, I like to think so." Her heart warmed. She knew her mother was smiling down on her from Heaven. "Where's Desiree?"

"She ran into the dress shop for a minute. I'm just out here cooling my heels and waiting for her," he replied. "So, when do you expect to open up for business?"

"It will be another month or so," she replied. She turned back and watched as Larry and his assistant got down from their ladders and folded them up.

"Is that good?" Larry asked her.

"It's absolutely perfect," she replied. "Thank you, Larry."

"No problem," he told her.

"It's quite eye-catching," George said.

"That's what we want," Larry said. "Let me know if there's anything else I can do for you, Miss Santori."

"I will, and again, thank you," Angelique said.

The sign men took their ladders and carried them

to their truck parked nearby. At that moment Desiree approached with a dress bag in her hand.

"Look, honey. Angelique is getting ready to open her shop. Isn't that terrific?" George said to her.

"Terrific," she said. "Hi, Angelique."

"Hi, Desiree," Angelique replied.

"I hope this is all very successful for you," Desiree said.

Angelique smiled at the beautiful woman next to George. "Thanks. I'm just eager to offer some help to people."

"Best of luck," Desiree said and then looked at George.

"I'm so darned happy to see this," he said to Angelique. "But I really shouldn't be surprised. I know how smart you are and how hard you've worked to make this happen."

Desiree tugged on his shirtsleeve. "Come on, honey. It's hot out here."

"Yeah, okay. We're on our way to the café to grab a bite to eat," George said.

"Enjoy," Angelique said and then watched as the two ambled on down the sidewalk.

She turned back around to look at her sign. A warm wash of pleasure swept over her. It was only the beginning, but finally it had begun. She was getting her dream and she couldn't be happier.

The warm pleasure suddenly iced over as the creepy feeling of being watched took its place. It was as palpable as a hot breath on the back of her neck or icy fingers walking up her spine.

She looked to the left and then slowly scanned to the right, but she saw nobody to give her pause. Still, she knew somebody was there…watching and waiting for the perfect opportunity to come after her again.

Chapter Ten

It had been a long week. Another fruitless, frustrating week of no clues and no leads in the two cases that haunted Daniel.

At the end of each day he dragged himself home and missed Angelique. The more he missed her, the more he realized the depths of his love for her. He loved her more than he'd ever loved anyone and the desire to build a life with her ached deep inside him.

But that wasn't what she needed from him. She'd made it clear on numerous occasions that she had no desire for a romantic relationship. That's what her lips said, but her touch told him something else, as did the glowing depths of her eyes when she gazed at him.

He believed she was in love with him, but Jason Webber had done such a number on her head…he had wounded her so badly, she refused to ever trust in love again. Could he get her to trust in him? Was it even possible that he could change her mind about love?

That was the question that burned bright inside him as he drove to her place on Saturday night. He couldn't wait to see her again, to spend time in her company. The week of not seeing her had been agony.

Each day he and his team beat the streets in an effort to bring her the answer as to who had killed her mother and who was after her. Each failure to do so ripped at his heart and very soul. And tonight, as usual, he was coming to her empty-handed.

It had been a little over a month since Mystique's murder. A month and they were no closer to solving the crime than they had been on the night she'd been found dead.

The most frustrating thing was they had two good suspects in Pierre and Charles, but there was no way to prove who was guilty and certainly not enough evidence to bring an indictment against either one of them.

It was another hot and sultry night as he got out of his car at the swamp's entrance. He walked quickly down the narrow trails that would take him to her shanty.

He felt like a schoolboy getting ready to have a date with the most popular girl in the school. At the same time, he felt like a man getting ready to claim the woman he loved.

Of course, he didn't intend to do that. The last thing he needed to do was tell her how very much he loved her. She wouldn't want to hear such a thing from him. It was just so difficult for him to keep his love for her locked inside him.

Finally, he reached her place and knocked on the door. "Angelique, it's me," he called out.

She opened the door and smiled at him warmly. "Good evening, Chief LeCroix," she said as she opened the door wide enough for him to enter.

"And good evening to you, Miss Santori," he replied. She gestured toward the sofa, where he sat.

"Can I get you something to drink?" she asked. She looked absolutely gorgeous in a pair of jeans and a dark purple sleeveless blouse.

"No, I'm good," he replied. He could smell the evocative scent that was specifically hers alone, the one that stirred him on so many levels.

She sank down next to him on the sofa. Her honey-hued eyes were warm as she gazed at him. "Daniel, I have to confess, I've really missed seeing you this week."

"And I really missed seeing you," he replied. "My evenings were quite lonely without you in them."

"Mine, too." She held his gaze for a long moment. Oh, it would be so easy for him to fall into the honey-depths of her eyes. His love for her simmered hot inside him, begging to be released.

He broke the eye contact and looked at a place just over her shoulder as he worked to get and keep his emotions under control. "Unfortunately, I come with no information for you again tonight." He released a heavy sigh and looked at her once again.

"You can only do what you can do," she replied.

"I know you and your sisters are disappointed by the lack of progress."

"I am…we are," she admitted. "But I also know it's a complicated case and you can't pull a rabbit out of a hat."

"Although Pierre and Charles are on my radar, it's possible another suspect might pop up," he said. "I know there are people who saw your mother under the cover of darkness that we haven't spoken to yet. But it's tough to identify them."

"I wish we would have found my mother's book. That would have made identifying everyone so much easier," she replied.

"It definitely would have been helpful," he agreed.

"I know how hard you're working on all this, Daniel." Once again, her gaze held his, and the intensity there half stole his breath away.

She leaned toward him and her lips parted as if in an invitation for a kiss. He wanted to kiss her. He so wanted to take her lips with his, but he didn't.

There was something in her gaze that told him a kiss would only be the beginning and it would lead to other things. As much as he'd love to make love to her again, he wouldn't. With his deep feelings for her burning so bright, so hot inside him, he couldn't do the casual thing with her anymore. He refused to be just one of the men she took to bed on a whim.

Instead, he leaned back from her. "The plan is that we'll keep digging and hopefully we'll get the murderer behind bars. On another note, have you thought of anyone who might have a beef with you?"

"No, and believe me I've been thinking about it almost all the time," she replied.

"Now, on a lighter note, I saw your new storefront. The sign is amazing, and it's already causing quite a bit of a buzz in town," he said.

She smiled, her pleasure obvious in her sparkling eyes. "Thanks. A buzz is a good thing, and things are moving right along. The interior has been painted and the shelving is all in place. I've been ordering some items for inventory and I'm starting to think about a grand opening."

"Your mother would be so proud of you. I'm so proud of you," he said. "I know how hard you've worked to make all this happen."

"Thanks, that means a lot."

"How soon before this grand opening of yours?" he asked.

"I'm thinking in a month or so. By then I should have everything in place for a successful opening."

"That's awesome, Angelique. We should plan a celebration on the night of the opening."

She reached out and took his hand in hers. "We could have a little celebration tonight." Her gaze was hot and the kind of celebration she had in mind was unmistakable.

He gazed at her for a long moment. "Angelique, I can't make love to you anymore," he finally said softly.

She tilted her head and looked at him in obvious curiosity. "Why not? Daniel, what's going on? I know you want me. I see it in your eyes, and I want you."

He drew in a deep breath. "Angelique, I can't be your casual roll in the hay. I can't be your casual anything. I… I can't because I'm deeply, madly in love with you." The words exploded out of him without his volition.

She stared at him, a look of horror on her features. "No, Daniel, you're mistaken," she finally said. "Take it back."

"I can't take it back," he replied. "Angelique, I'm

completely in love with you, and I think if you look deep in your heart, you'll realize you're in love with me, too."

"I'm not. Don't say that. You know I don't do love." She jumped up off the sofa and glared at him. "I warned you. I told you in a million different ways that I don't want love or a relationship in my life."

He got up from the sofa as well, his heart beating an uneven rhythm as he faced her. "Are you forever going to allow fear to dictate your life? Are you always going to allow Jason Webber to keep you a prisoner?"

Her cheeks flushed with color. "Men lie and they cheat."

"No. Jason lied and cheated, but he isn't all men." He reached out and placed his palms on either side of her beautiful face. "I'm not Jason," he exclaimed passionately. "I don't lie and I would never cheat. I love you, Angelique. I want to marry you. I want you to be my wife and the mother of my children." He dropped his hands to his sides. "I want us to build a happy life together."

"Stop it…please just stop it," she said as tears filled her eyes. "I don't want to hear any more. I don't love you, Daniel. I don't."

Daniel drew in another deep breath and released it slowly. "I'm sorry, Angelique. I certainly don't want to hurt you in any way. That's the very last thing I wanted to do. I guess I'd hoped you…well, it doesn't matter now."

He shouldn't have told her how he felt about her. He should have just kept it locked inside him until another time. He should have just kept his mouth shut. Now he feared that things were forever ruined between them.

"I'm sorry, Daniel. I'm so sorry I can't be the woman you want or need," she said.

"But, Angelique, you are that woman," he protested. "You're exactly what I want and need in my life."

She shook her head. "I'm not, because I don't intend to ever marry."

He stared at her in frustration. "That's a damned shame, Angelique. Because I'm the man who would have cherished you. I'm the man who would have loved you better than any other man on the face of the earth."

There was nothing more he could say. He'd poured out his heart and soul to her, and it wasn't enough. He wasn't enough. The ball was now in her court, and she'd decided she didn't want to play. His heart ached with a deep pain.

"I promise I won't speak to you of this again," he finally said.

"Thank you," she replied softly.

"Now, I think it's past time I leave." He headed toward the front door and she walked just behind him. When he reached the door, he pulled it open and then turned back to her.

"I'll be here next Saturday night if you still want me to make the check-ins," he said.

"Next Saturday will be fine," she replied stiffly.

"Then I'll just say good night."

"Good night, Daniel."

With that, he walked out the door and into the darkness of the night. He'd really believed she was in love with him. He still believed she was in love with him. But he couldn't break through her strong defenses. Or was it really possible that she didn't love him?

It didn't matter now. None of it mattered. All he knew for sure was that his heart ached with a deep pain he'd never felt before. He had a feeling it was going to take a very long time for him to get over loving Angelique.

ONCE DANIEL WAS GONE, Angelique sank down on her sofa and began to cry. His words of love had been such a shock. Oh, she'd known that he cared about her, just like she cared for him. But she hadn't realized the depths of his feelings for her.

And she was in love with him. Although she had insisted to him that she wasn't, that had been a lie. She loved him like she'd never loved a man before, but it scared her. She was so afraid of getting hurt again.

It was better to keep herself safe by not reaching out to embrace his love rather than to grasp hold of it and then be hurt. She cried for several long minutes and then got up from the sofa and got ready for bed.

She wanted to escape the emotions that filled her head and heart. She wanted to escape into the sweet oblivion of sleep and hopefully she would sleep without dreams.

THE NEXT MORNING, she was meeting her sisters for breakfast at the café. The heartache she felt still resonated through her as she dressed for the day in a pair of jeans and a hot pink T-shirt.

Once it was time, she left her shanty and headed toward the swamp entrance. Dominique and Monique were already at her car, waiting for her.

They greeted her brightly, and then they all got in the car and Angelique drove toward town. The topic of conversation was Angelique's store.

"You do realize you're going to have to hire a couple of people to work for you," Monique said from the back seat. "There's no way you can work all the hours you'll want to be open by yourself."

"Yeah, I figure I'll need at least two, maybe three, other people to work for me. I'm going to post on social media and put an ad in the paper. Then hopefully in the next week or so I'll have some people to interview," Angelique replied.

It was a relief to talk about the store and nothing more. The last thing she wanted to talk about was anything that had to do with Daniel or love.

"You should order some cute T-shirts with a logo on the front for your employees to wear," Dominique said. "Purple shirts would be nice."

"That's a great idea," Angelique replied. "I'll definitely check into that."

They continued to talk about the store until they arrived at the café. Once they were seated in a booth and as they waited for their orders to arrive, Monique filled them in on who had been in the dress shop and who had bought what. "Laura Sanders came in and bought the cutest hot pink pants and a blouse that was hot pink and red. She's going to look great in it."

"You always know exactly what to show the customers to make a sale," Angelique said. "Maybe I should hire you to work in my store."

"Ha, sorry, sis, but you couldn't afford me," Monique retorted with a giggle.

The conversation remained light and easy as they ate. Still, Angelique couldn't help but think about Daniel and what had happened between the two of them the night before.

There was a deep sadness inside her and she didn't quite understand it. She'd made the choice to step away from Daniel. It wasn't like she wanted the love that he'd offered her…did she?

"Angelique!"

She suddenly became aware that Dominique was talking to her. "Yeah?"

"Where did you just go? I've called your name three times," Dominique said.

"Sorry, I just zoned out for a minute," Angelique replied.

"I was asking what Daniel had to say about the investigations," Dominique said. "Anything new?"

"No. Things have pretty much stalled out, but I know he's working hard to get a solve," Angelique replied. "I just saw him last night. He stopped in to give me an update." A wealth of emotion suddenly rose inside her and she quickly looked down at her plate as tears misted her vision.

"Hey, Angelique…what's going on?" Monique asked softly.

Angelique shook her head and drew in a deep

breath. "I can't talk about it right now," she managed to say.

"Then are we ready to go?" Dominique asked.

"I'm ready," Monique said and Angelique echoed it.

Dominique waved for their tab and minutes later the three left the café. "Okay, spill it," Dominique commanded the moment they were back in the car.

"Yeah, tell us what's going on with you," Monique said. "You're obviously upset about something."

Angelique hesitated a moment before replying. "He told me he's in love with me," she finally said, and tears once again pressed hot and seeped down her cheeks.

"Who? Daniel?" Dominique asked.

Angelique nodded her head. "He told me he's in love with me and wants to marry me."

"And that's a bad thing?" Dominique asked.

"You aren't in love with him?" Monique asked.

"No, I am crazy in love with him," Angelique confessed.

"Then what's the problem?" Dominique asked.

"Me… I'm the problem." Angelique tightened her hands on the steering wheel. "You both know how I feel about relationships. I don't want to be in love, and I don't want him to be in love with me."

"Oh, Angelique," Monique said in dismay. "You can't let your experience with Jason ruin the rest of your life. He was a piece of dirt, but that doesn't mean Daniel is."

"Monique and I should have hunted Jason down and beat his butt for what he did to you," Dominique said fervently. "Or maybe we should beat your butt for being so damned stubborn about all this."

"Angelique, if you truly love him and he truly loves you, then you shouldn't let this pass you by. You'll always be haunted by the what-ifs. What if Daniel is a man who won't lie or cheat on you? What if he is the kind of stand-up man who can truly make you happy?"

"Angelique, don't allow fear to rule your life. Don't let your fear ruin your chance at love," Monique said. "I always believed you were the big sister who was afraid of nothing."

"Okay, enough," Angelique said as she parked the car and turned off the engine.

"We just want to see you happy, sis," Dominique said.

"I know, but I hope you both will support me no matter what decision I make," Angelique said.

"You know you always have our support," Monique said.

The three got out of the car and headed into the swamp. It was a quiet walk, and Angelique was grateful for the silence. Her head was spinning with all the thoughts and emotions that filled it.

When she got back to her shanty, she spent the rest of the afternoon working, which kept all other thoughts away. But the minute she closed her computer, thoughts of Daniel filled her head once again.

He'd been a constant in her life for a little over a month. She had enjoyed each and every moment she'd spent with him. The nightly visits had fast-tracked their closeness to each other.

Last night he'd looked so handsome in his jeans and a white polo shirt. She'd wanted him last night. She'd wanted him to kiss her passionately and she'd wanted him to make love with her again. It had surprised and confused her when he hadn't responded to her obvious openness.

Why had he ruined everything with his talk of loving her? They'd had a wonderful relationship going with things being casual between them. She would have been satisfied if things had remained the status quo. Or was it possible a time would come when she wanted more from him?

She was so damned confused now. She was torn between love and fear, torn between want and the bad taste Jason had left in her mouth.

She called it a day early and got into bed. As she remembered Daniel spending the night with her, her heart squeezed tight. She had felt so safe that night. It had felt so right to fall asleep in his arms.

Could she trust him to love her forever? Could she believe that he would never lie to her or cheat? She closed her eyes and the night sounds of the swamp slowly soothed her.

She must have fallen asleep for she jerked awake suddenly. Instantly a surge of adrenaline coursed through her. She grabbed her knife from beneath her pillow and then sat up and listened.

Had her attacker come back? Was Angelique no longer alone in the shanty? Her heart beat frantically. From the moonlight drifting in the window, she could see there was nothing amiss in her bedroom.

But what about the rest of the house? Had her attacker somehow found a way in? There was still wood in the window that had been broken before, so an intruder could no longer break the glass and get to the door lock. She slowly slid out of the bed. On shaking legs, she moved to the bedroom doorway.

She hadn't heard anything, but something had awakened her. Drawing a deep breath, she twirled out of the bedroom and into the living room.

It was darker there, but she saw nothing to give her pause. She then moved into the kitchen and there was nobody there, either. She checked her mother's room and the smaller room and there was nobody there… nobody anywhere.

She went back into the living room and turned on the lanterns that would light up the room. She then sank down on the sofa and released a deep tremulous sigh.

It must have been a dream that had awakened her in such a state. Another attack was always on her mind. Thank goodness, tonight it had been a false alarm.

She didn't know how long she sat on the sofa, but eventually she got up and went back into her bedroom. She kept all the lanterns lit, including the one on her nightstand.

She finally fell asleep with thoughts of being wrapped in Daniel's arms.

Chapter Eleven

Early on Wednesday morning Daniel sat at his desk and sipped his coffee as a million thoughts whirled through his head. It had been four days since he'd told Angelique that he was in love with her...four long days since she'd broken his heart into a million pieces by not loving him back.

During those four days, he and his officers had worked the cases with no further information to lead them to the killer and Angelique's attacker. They had reinterviewed people and spoke again to individuals they knew had visited Mystique for one reason or another.

Even though he believed Pierre was still the most likely suspect, that didn't mean he stopped the investigation. They had brought in a lot of the other gator hunters to see if Pierre might have confessed to one of them, but nobody had heard any kind of a confession from Mystique's off-again, on-again lover.

In the quiet moments of his days, his thoughts filled with Angelique. His heart positively ached with his love for her. He'd heard the songs about heartbreak and unrequited love, but he'd never felt the utter despair of those emotions until now.

At eight o'clock that morning when Luke and Clay arrived for work, he led them back to the murder room. "I want us to start at the beginning and go through each and every report and interview to see if we've somehow missed something," he explained.

The three of them settled at the round table in the room. "Clay, why don't you go through the crime scene information and Luke, you can start by reading the interviews. If you find anything that sounds off, or if we failed to follow up on things, let me know. We'll keep a list of anything that needs to be checked further."

"Sounds like a plan," Clay said and Luke agreed.

More than anything Daniel wanted to find the killer. If she refused to accept his love, he could at least give her peace of mind by giving her the killer's name.

The three of them worked until eleven, and then they decided to go to the café for their lunch break. "So far, I feel like our investigation has been pretty solid," Luke said once they were in Daniel's car.

"We still have quite a bit to get through," Daniel replied.

"I'm hoping something will stand out…something we haven't considered before."

"It's a crummy day out," Clay observed.

The clouds overhead were thick and gray, causing a gloomy overcast that reflected Daniel's mood. "Yeah, I heard we're supposed to get some rain later," Luke said.

"Maybe the rain will dissipate some of the heavy

humidity and heat," Daniel replied. It was safe to talk about the weather. He hadn't told Clay or Luke what was going on in his personal life. They had no idea their boss was sporting a huge broken heart.

They reached the café, where he parked, and the three of them got out of the car. Once inside they found an empty booth and sat down.

Luke grabbed a menu. "I don't know why, but I'm starving today."

"Yeah, me too," Clay replied.

Daniel had no real appetite. He hadn't had one since last Saturday night. "Good afternoon, gentlemen." Dominique appeared at their booth. The sight of her caused an aching pain to squeeze his chest. She looked so much like her older sister.

"What can I get for you all today?" she asked.

Luke ordered the meat loaf special, Clay ordered the fried fish platter and Daniel ordered a bacon cheeseburger. They all ordered sodas.

"I'll be right back with those drinks," Dominique said and then left the side of their booth.

Almost immediately Nola Fontenot appeared at their booth. "Chief LeCroix," she began as she twisted her plump hands together in front of her. "Is there any news on Mystique's murderer?" she asked.

"We're still in the middle of our investigation," he replied, wishing the answer was different.

"I believe Pierre killed her. He couldn't stand not having her. Can't you arrest him and get him behind bars? I hate to see him walking around free while my best friend is dead and gone," Nola said.

"It's not that easy, Mrs. Fontenot," Daniel replied.

"Well, it should be that easy. Mystique was a wonderful woman, and I miss her every single day," Nola said.

"I know the two of you were good friends and I'm sorry for your loss, but we're working as hard as we can to see that the person who killed her is arrested and charged with her murder. The last thing we'd want to do is arrest an innocent man," Daniel said.

At that moment Dominique returned with their drinks, and Nola went back to her own table across the room. "The good thing is if Pierre is our man, I don't see him killing anyone else," Luke said.

"Yeah, it could be worse with some crazed murderer killing other woman in the same manner," Clay replied.

Daniel listened to his two officers talk about the case, and then their conversation turned to their personal lives. "How are you and Anita getting along," Luke asked Clay.

Clay and Anita Cook had been dating for the past couple of months. Anita was a pretty, sweet woman who worked as a nurse at the small hospital in town.

"Things are going good," Clay replied. "Although between my work hours and hers, we don't get to see each other as often as we'd like to. When are you going to find some nice woman?" he asked Luke.

"Who knows? I'm in the market to find one," Luke replied and then looked across the table at Daniel. "And I think we all know who has Daniel's heart. It's evident every time he says her name."

"Unfortunately, she's not interested in having a relationship with me," Daniel replied, the words causing his chest to squeeze tight.

"Well, that's a real bummer," Clay said.

"Here we are," Dominique said as she arrived with their food. She placed the plates in front of them and then smiled. "Is there anything else I can get for you?"

"No, I think this will do it. Thanks, Dominique," Daniel said.

She smiled and hesitated a moment. "Uh, before you leave, could I have a private word with you?" she asked Daniel.

He looked at her in surprise. "Sure," he replied.

"Okay, in the meantime enjoy your meals," she said and then left the booth.

"What's that all about?" Clay asked.

"I don't have a clue," Daniel replied. He was definitely intrigued and wondered what Dominique could want to discuss with him. Maybe she'd thought of somebody who had a beef with her sister. That would be great. More than anything Daniel wanted the person who had attacked Angelique in jail.

As they ate, they talked about mundane things like the weather and things that were going on in town. There were always programs going on at the community center to keep the kids from running amok in the summer days.

It was one of the best things that Mayor Ralph Dupree had implemented during his time in office. Many of the children participated in the programs, and it kept them safe and off the streets when they weren't in school.

They finished eating and paid, and then Clay and Luke headed on outside to the car while Daniel waited for Dominique. She walked over to him and pulled him into an office just off the kitchen area.

"I only have a minute or two," she said. "But I wanted to let you know that Angelique is totally in love with you. And if you truly love her, you need to keep telling her that. Eventually, I really believe you'll break through to her. She's just so afraid of being hurt again, but she told us she's madly in love with you."

Daniel wanted to believe her. He wanted to believe her so badly. "Thanks, Dominique," he replied.

"We both know how stubborn she can be, but she told us she's deeply in love with you, so please don't give up on her, Daniel. And now I have to get back to work."

"Thanks again, Dominique," he replied.

She nodded and then hurried out of the office. Daniel left the office, too. While she headed back to the dining room floor, he went out the front door and to the car where Clay and Luke waited for him.

"Everything okay?" Clay asked.

"Everything is fine," Daniel replied. He didn't intend to share with his buddies what Dominique had said to him.

As he drove back to the station, Dominique's words whirled around and around in his head. Did he have the emotional stamina to keep telling Angelique he loved her? Even knowing she might deny loving him over and over again?

With his heart still badly broken from his last encounter with her, he wasn't sure he had the answer to that.

THURSDAY EVENING ANGELIQUE picked at the salad she'd made herself for dinner. Nothing tasted good to her. She hadn't had much of an appetite since last Saturday night when Daniel had professed his love for her.

Could she trust him to love her through thick and thin? Could she believe that he would never lie to her or cheat? She knew without a doubt that he was a stand-up kind of guy. So, what was she so afraid of?

Heartache? She felt that already. As usual she'd missed him through the past week. She had no idea what to expect from him on Saturday night. There was no question that things had changed between them with his vows of his love for her. So, how uncomfortable would things be between them now.

She wished they could go back in time, and she wouldn't have had to examine her emotions where Daniel was concerned. She wished she didn't know about his love for her. More importantly she wished she didn't know about her love for him. Things would be so much less complicated then.

She finished eating and cleaned up the kitchen then went into the living room and sank down on the sofa. Between her work and getting things together for the shop, at least she'd managed to stay busy and that had helped keep thoughts of Daniel away.

However, each time there was a moment of silence, every time her mind wasn't occupied with other things, her thoughts filled with the man she'd fallen in love with. Was he really the hero she'd once yearned to find?

A knock fell on her door and quickened her heartbeat. Was it Daniel? Had there been a break in the case? Why else would he be here on a Thursday when they'd agreed to Saturday night check-ins? She jumped up off the sofa and hurried to answer the door. She paused before opening it. Normally Daniel yelled out to her that it was him.

She grabbed her knife. "Who is it?" she called out.

"Angelique, it's Desiree," the feminine voice answered.

Desiree? Angelique put her knife back on the end table and then opened the door.

"Desiree," she said, surprised to see the tall, beautiful woman there.

"Hi, Angelique. I was wondering if I could come in and have a quick chat with you," Desiree said with a smile.

"Of course." Angelique opened her door wider to allow her entry. What on earth could George's girlfriend need to talk about with her?

"Please, have a seat." Angelique gestured toward the sofa. "Can I get you anything to drink?"

"No thanks, I'm good." Desiree sat on the sofa and Angelique sat in a chair facing her.

"What's going on?" she asked curiously.

"I wanted to talk to you about George," Desiree said.

"George? What about him?"

Desiree leaned forward. "You know his birthday is coming up real soon and I'm planning a surprise party for him."

"Oh, I'm sure he'll love that," Angelique replied.

"I was just wondering if maybe you could help me with a guest list," Desiree said.

"I'll certainly try, although I imagine you know more of George's friends than I do. George and I haven't exactly stayed in touch."

Desiree leaned forward even more. "I am so in love with that man." Her dark eyes blazed with emotion. "George is the man I want in my life forever."

"From what I've seen, George appears to be deeply in love with you, too," Angelique replied. What did any of this have to do with her? Why was Desiree really here? Desiree didn't need Angelique to help with any guest list for a birthday party. So, what was really going on here?

"Yes, I believe George loves me, but he won't completely be mine until you're out of the way."

Angelique's heart stepped up its rhythm. "I don't understand," she replied. "George and I don't have any kind of a relationship."

"That may be true, but you aren't out of his head. Every time your name comes up, he talks about how beautiful you are, how smart and what a wonderful woman you are. Angelique this and Angelique that... I have to listen to him talking about your virtues all the damned time."

"I… I'm sorry to hear that." Angelique wasn't sure what else to say.

"I truly believe he won't completely be over you until you're gone for good." She rose from the sofa and pulled a wicked-looking knife from her pocket. "So, I'm here to make sure that happens."

Angelique jumped to her feet and grabbed at her own knife. She stared at Desiree in horror. "So, it was you…you broke in here before."

"I did. I went to a lot of trouble that night to get to you, but you won that round. I thought about trying to break into your back door, and then I realized I could just knock on the door and come right in. Nobody will even know I was here." She laughed, the wicked sound causing a chill to walk up Angelique's spine.

"Desiree, it doesn't have to be this way." She couldn't help but notice that the knife Desiree held in her hand was twice the size of Angelique's.

"It does have to be this way. Once you're dead, then George won't be talking about you anymore. His heart will finally be free to completely love me and me only."

With a sudden swift movement, Desiree came at Angelique, stabbing out with her knife. Angelique managed to evade the thrusts as she stumbled backward. If she could just get to the potbelly stove like she had last time then she could pull the poker once again.

Instead, Desiree moved so that her back was to the stove and there was no way for Angelique to get to the poker. "You don't get to win this time," she said.

"Desiree, you don't want to do this," Angelique cried out. "You aren't a killer."

"Oh, but I am," Desiree replied, her eyes burning with hatred...with pure evil. "I will kill so I have George all to myself. It will give me great pleasure to kill you." Once again, she leaped out at Angelique, and the knifepoint managed to pierce Angelique in her arm.

Pain instantly filled her at the point of contact and she jabbed back in an effort to move Desiree back from her. Terror sliced through her as she recognized this was a fight for her very life.

Somehow, someway, she needed to get the knife away from Desiree. Otherwise, with Desiree's longer arms and her bigger knife, eventually she would be able to complete a killing stab.

Angelique kicked out, in an effort to keep distance between herself and Desiree. "Did you kill my mother?" she managed to gasp out.

Desiree's eyes widened slightly. "No. I wouldn't mess with the voodoo queen." She jabbed out again. "And I wouldn't have come at you with her still alive."

Angelique remembered the note left on her door, indicating that the person who was after her had been afraid of her mother. So, Desiree wasn't her mother's murderer, but she intended to murder Angelique. "Did you leave the note on my door?" Angelique asked.

"I did. I wanted you to feel fear."

Jab...weave...dodge. The two women performed a macabre dance of impending death. Angelique managed to cut Desiree's arm and Desiree sliced across

Angelique's shoulder. Both women were bloody as they continued to fight.

Angelique managed to gain some distance from her attacker and remembering the note left on her door, she raised her arms up in the air and began chanting some gibberish.

"What are you doing?" Desiree asked, the words coming out of her on gasps from their exertions. "What's that you're saying?"

"I am my mother's daughter, born on the seventh night of the seventh month beneath a black moon and I am putting a curse on you," Angelique said and then continued mouthing more gibberish. "I am the new voodoo queen in town."

"Stop it," Desiree said frantically. "Stop it right now." She stood still, horror on her features and at that moment Angelique kicked out. She connected with Desiree's hand and her knife went flying through the air and landed some feet away from her.

Desiree scrambled across the floor like a fast-moving lizard. She grabbed the knife once again and then leaped at Angelique. Desiree hit her midsection and knocked her down.

Angelique fell back, her breath exploding out of her as she crashed the back of her head against the floor. At the same time Desiree jumped on top of her and drove her knife into Angelique's chest. Pain seared through her and a deep sob escaped her. Oh God, she was going to die. Desiree was really going to kill her.

"Die, bitch, die!" Desiree screamed as she raised the knife for another killing blow.

At that moment the front door slammed open and Daniel strode in. He instantly pulled his gun. "Drop the knife, Desiree," he yelled. "Drop it now, or I'll shoot you."

Desiree hesitated for a long moment, and then she finally tossed the knife to the side and rolled off Angelique and to her feet. "She tried to kill me, Chief. I just stopped by to have a friendly chat with her about George's birthday party, and all of a sudden, she went totally nuts on me. I stabbed her in self-defense."

Daniel wasted no time. He quickly handcuffed Desiree and sat her on the sofa. "Don't move," he commanded, and then he rushed to Angelique's side. The pain in her chest nearly stole all her breath away.

His gaze was dark as it lingered on her. He crouched down next to her. "Angelique…honey. Don't try to move," he said to her. He grabbed his radio and called for backup and medical.

"She's nuts," Desiree said. "Who treats a guest this way? Out of nowhere she came at me with a knife, told me she was going to kill me and bury me deep in the swamp where nobody would ever find my body."

"Why did you come here? What exactly did you want to discuss with her?" he asked. He remained next to Angelique, who was in excruciating pain.

"George's birthday is coming up and I just wanted to see if she wanted to help me throw him a surprise birthday party," she replied.

"Sh…she is the one who attacked me be…before," Angelique managed to gasp out. "S… She wanted to k…kill me."

"Don't try to talk," he said to her. She saw the concern on his features. Heck, she was concerned for herself. It was getting harder and harder for her to breathe and the dark edges of unconsciousness encroached closer and closer.

The darkness finally overtook her. Her eyes slowly closed and she knew no more.

Chapter Twelve

Horror swept through Daniel as he realized Angelique had fallen unconscious. He was afraid to try to help her as in doing so he didn't know if he'd hurt her more than she'd already been hurt. And how badly was she hurt? He could see the blood on her arm and shoulder, but more horrifying was the blood on her chest, indicating that she'd been stabbed there. How deep was the wound?

Desiree continued to profess her innocence and insisted she had acted in self-defense. But Daniel knew the truth and as Desiree continued to talk, the reason for the attacks on Angelique became clear.

It was all because George often spoke highly of Angelique. It was sick and twisted and right now his biggest fear was that Desiree had been successful in her desire to kill Angelique.

Thank goodness help arrived fairly quickly. Luke and Clay showed up at the same time that the EMTs came into the shanty. The EMTs immediately got to work stabilizing Angelique. Daniel watched them, his heart in his throat as they put an oxygen mask on her and got an IV going. Then they strapped her to a board and carried her out.

"Go," Luke said to Daniel and pointed to the shanty door. "Clay and I and a couple of the other men can get Desiree to the jail and we'll process the scene here. You go on to the hospital. That's where you belong."

"Thanks. I know you all can handle things here." With that, Daniel left the shanty and hurried after the men who carried Angelique.

How bad were her wounds? Both women had been covered in blood but it was the blood on Angelique's chest that scared the very hell out of him. She'd been stabbed and he had no idea what damage had been done. She had to be okay, she just had to be.

It seemed to take forever to get through the swamp, but finally he was in his car and following behind the ambulance with its swirling red and blue lights and blaring siren.

She was still unconscious when they arrived at the hospital, where she was whisked away into the emergency room. Daniel checked in at the front desk and let the receptionist know he wanted to see the doctor the minute he was available.

He then sank down in one of the beige plastic chairs in the waiting room. He leaned his head back and closed his eyes as his mind replayed that moment when he'd walked into the shanty and had seen Desiree on top of Angelique, her knife raised to deliver a killing blow.

Thank God, he'd entered the shanty when he had. If he'd been a moment longer, Angelique would have been stabbed again. With Dominique's words ringing in his ears, he'd decided to make an impromptu visit to Angelique's. And thank God he had heard screaming coming from inside the shanty. He'd been lucky that the door had been unlocked. Had it been locked, Angelique would be dead.

Now all he could do was pray that Angelique was going to survive this night of horror. She had to be all right. She just had to be. His heart couldn't stand it if she wasn't okay.

A long hour passed and then another one and finally Dr. Gregory Harmon came out to talk to him. Daniel stood at the sight of the older man, who was also Daniel's own personal doctor.

"Dr. Harmon…how is she?"

"She's going to be just fine," he replied. The words caused a rush of shuddery relief to sweep through Daniel. "She required stitches on her shoulder and more stitches due to an arm wound. The biggest issue she has is the wound in her chest. The tip of the knife managed to hit her lung. The wound is small and so it's a wait and see situation. I'm hoping the lung will go ahead and heal itself. If it doesn't, then I'll have to go in to surgically to repair it. But right now things look good."

"When will you know if surgery is necessary?" Daniel asked.

"Within the next twenty-four to forty-eight hours," Dr. Harmon replied. "Needless to say she's going to be my guest here for the next couple of nights."

"Can I see her?" Daniel asked anxiously.

The doctor frowned. “I would prefer she have no visitors tonight. She was in a mild state of shock when she first got here, but I now have her resting comfortably and I’d like to keep it that way.”

“Understood,” Daniel said with a bit of disappointment. “Can you tell me what room she’s in so I can see her tomorrow?”

“She’s in room 103,” the doctor replied.

Minutes later Daniel stepped out of the hospital and met Dominique and Monique coming in. “Is she all right?” Monique asked urgently, tears glimmering in her eyes.

“She’s going to be just fine,” Daniel replied and then told them everything the doctor had told him.

“I can’t believe it was Desiree all this time,” Dominique said. “I would have never guessed she was behind the attacks on Angelique.”

“I never liked that woman,” Monique added. “So, we can’t see Angelique tonight?”

“The doctor has said no visitors for the night, but I’m sure you’ll be able to see her first thing in the morning,” he replied. “When I called you both to let you know what had happened, I didn’t know you wouldn’t be able to see her.”

“We just appreciate you calling us,” Dominique replied. Her eyes also shimmered with a hint of tears. “Thank you for saving her, Daniel.”

“We love her so much,” Monique said.

“I… I love her, too. That’s why I went to the shanty this evening…to tell her again how much I love her,” he confessed.

He cleared his throat, surprised by the wealth of emotion that suddenly threatened to overtake him. "Anyway, I'm just on my way back to the shanty to clear it since it's a crime scene again."

"Keep loving her, Daniel," Dominique said softly. "She deserves the love of a good man like you."

Minutes later as he drove back to the shanty, he thought about Dominique's words. What Dominique didn't realize was he couldn't stop loving Angelique even if he tried.

He was in too deep, and her name had become permanently etched into his heart, into his very soul. He'd pour his heart out to her tomorrow and the day after that. He'd tell Angelique how much he loved her for however long it took.

But maybe Dominique was wrong and Angelique truly didn't love him. Doubts took up residency in his mind. Maybe he could pour his heart out to her for a hundred days and she still wouldn't accept his love because she didn't want it, because she really didn't love him. With this depressing thought in mind, he pulled up at the swamp entrance and headed in to the shanty.

They worked processing the scene at Angelique's place until after midnight, even though there wasn't much of anything there to collect. Pictures were taken, and then Daniel spent some time cleaning up the blood from the braided rug. The last thing he wanted was for Angelique to come home and have to see the blood spilled.

He found her purse in the corner of the sofa and grabbed it. She would probably need it before she left the hospital. Finally, he locked the shanty door and walked out to his car.

Driving home, the moon was nearly full overhead and his thoughts were consumed by Angelique and how close she'd come to death on this night.

Once home, it took him forever to get to sleep. Images and emotions from the night played in his head… in his heart, keeping sleep at bay. He wasn't sure what time he finally fell asleep. But despite the long night, he was at the hospital by eight the next morning.

The hospital hallways smelled of fresh coffee and breakfast foods as he strode to her room. He turned into room 103 and there she was…looking small and vulnerable in the big hospital bed.

"Daniel," she said with a wan smile.

"Well, you look better today than you did last night," he said and pulled a chair up to her bedside.

"I wish I could say I feel better today, but I have pain where I didn't even know I had body parts," she replied.

The white bandage on her arm reminded him of the last time she'd sported such a bandage. Both injuries inflicted by Desiree at different times. Although he couldn't see it, he also knew she had another bandage on her shoulder and one on her chest wound as well.

The thought of her wounds made him angry as hell. He would have never thought of Desiree being the perp in the attacks against Angelique. If Desiree hadn't been caught in the act, she would have gotten away with murder.

"I hate it that you're in so much pain," he said.

"The good news is the doctor tells me my lung is healing itself and I probably won't need any surgery," she added. "They pulled me off the oxygen early this morning."

"That's great news," he replied. "I brought your purse from your shanty." He set it on the foot of her bed. "I figured you might need it while you were here."

"Thank you, I appreciate it." She stared at him for a long moment and her eyes began to tear up a bit. "You saved my life, Daniel. She was going to kill me, and if you hadn't stopped her when you did, she would have succeeded."

"Hey, no tears allowed." He reached out and drew her hand into his. "All's well that ends well, right?"

"Right," she replied with a small laugh. "We Santori women are a tough bunch."

"Thank God. And Desiree is going to jail for a very long time," he said. There were so many things he wanted to say to her, but for the moment he stayed professional.

"Unfortunately, right now I need to get an official statement from you. Are you up to doing that now?" he asked.

She nodded. "Okay, might as well get it over with." For the next fifteen minutes or so she told him about Desiree coming to visit and then pulling a knife.

Daniel occasionally stopped her to ask a question, and then she finished up with her on the floor and Desiree on top of her.

He was just about to spill his heart to her again

when a hospital aide pushed in a cart with her breakfast tray on it.

"Good morning," the gray-haired woman greeted them. "I've got some scrambled eggs and bacon for our patient. There's also coffee and orange juice." She pulled a table across Angelique's lap and then placed the tray of food on top of it. "Sorry, Chief LeCroix, I've got nothing for you."

"That's okay," he replied. "I ate before I came."

"Enjoy, honey," she said to Angelique, and then she left the room.

"Eat it while it's warm," he urged her.

"I'm really not overly hungry," she said.

"At least try to eat a little," he replied.

Dutifully she picked up a piece of toast and took a bite. "Eat some of those eggs. Don't make me play the airplane game with you," he said and was rewarded by her laughter.

"You're still such a goof," she said.

"I'm only a goof with you," he replied. "Angelique…"

George Trahan strode into the room. "Angelique… oh God, Angelique, I'm so sorry." He walked to the opposite side of her bed and pulled up a chair next to her. "Angelique, I had no idea… I didn't know what she was planning to do to you."

The man looked utterly miserable as he raked a hand through his hair and gazed at her. "I still can't believe what she did. I can't believe I was sleeping with a monster."

"It's okay, George. I don't blame you for what happened," Angelique replied.

"But I should have seen something… I should have somehow stopped it before it even started," he replied. "I'm just so damned sorry." He appeared to be on the verge of tears.

"George, really it's okay. You have nothing to apologize for," she said.

"I just wanted to stop by to make sure you're going to be okay and to tell you I had no idea what she was up to. I still just can't believe this happened. I thought I knew Desiree, but I sure didn't know she was capable of something like this."

He got up from the chair. "I just… I needed to see you and now I'll just leave you to your breakfast."

As he left the room, Dominique and Monique came in. Daniel had come to the hospital hoping to declare his undying love for Angelique, but there was too much traffic and the mood wasn't right. He stayed another few minutes, and then he left to head to work.

One case was solved, but he still had a murder investigation to get back to. It was six o'clock when he left the police station and headed back to the hospital.

As always, he was eager to see her. He whirled into the room and stopped in his tracks. She was a sleeping beauty in the bed. Her hair was a cloud of darkness against the white pillowcase and her features were relaxed in slumber.

The last thing he wanted to do was wake her up. He slowly backed out of the room. Maybe a hospital wasn't the right place to have a romantic interlude. Hopefully the right time would come very soon, but for now he decided the best thing to do was wait.

ANGELIQUE AWAKENED EARLY on her third day in the hospital. She felt well rested and much better than she had since the night she'd been brought in. She still had pain, but that was to be expected. It was going to take her some time to completely heal from Desiree's attack.

It was finally over. She no longer had to look over her shoulder or be afraid to leave her shanty again. The person who had wanted her dead was now behind bars and according to Daniel she would be there for a very long time. There was no more reason for Angelique to be afraid.

She stared out the nearby window, where the sun was bright, promising another hot and humid day. She was hoping she would be released today. She felt as if she'd been granted a new life and she was eager now to go out and live it.

She was also eager to see Daniel again. She hadn't seen him since the morning he had taken her report. Her heart squeezed tight as she thought of him. At least he no longer had to be concerned about the attacks on her.

All he had to deal with now was her mother's murder. Would he still be willing to meet with her to keep her updated on the case? Would he still want to spend evenings with her just visiting and enjoying each other's company? Did he still believe himself in love with her or had he realized it wasn't love after all.

It was just after noon when the doctor came in to see her. "The good news is you're healing up quite nicely," he told her.

"And what's the bad news?" she asked.

"The bad news is it looks like we'll have to do without your presence here because I'm releasing you to go home today," he said with a smile.

"That's wonderful news," she replied. "I'm so ready to get back to my life."

"I'm releasing you with the instructions that you get plenty of rest and don't push yourself. Your body is still healing, and if you don't behave yourself you'll be right back here with me," he said.

"I promise I'll take care of myself," she replied. "When can I leave?"

"All I need to do is write up the orders, and then I'll send the nurse in and we'll get you on your way."

"Thank you, Dr. Harmon." The moment he left the room, she got on the landline on the stand next to her bed and called Dominique to get a ride home. Her cell phone was in her purse, but it was dead. She also asked that Dominique bring her some clean clothes to put on. The blouse she'd worn on the night of the attack was ruined. Thank goodness the two sisters wore the same size.

It was forty-five minutes later when she walked out of the hospital doors with Dominique at her side. She'd had a quick shower and was now clad in a pair of Dominique's jeans and a button-up sleeveless red blouse.

"I'll bet you're eager to get home," Dominique said.

"I am. I have a lot of things to do to get the shop up and running," Angelique replied.

"Don't overwork yourself, sis. You're not back to

one hundred percent yet and won't be for a while. You've been through a terrible trauma."

"I know, but thank God I'm here to talk about it," Angelique replied. As she thought of those moments of fighting with Desiree, even now a residual fear worried through her.

They reached Dominique's car and got inside, then headed toward the swamp entrance. "Are you off work today?" Angelique asked.

"No, I'm working the evening shift. Isn't it nice that you don't have to be afraid anymore?"

"That is nice," Angelique replied. "I still can't believe it was Desiree who was after me. In a million years I would have never guessed she was the one behind the attack. Thank God it's all finally over."

As they continued on, Angelique told her sister about the people who had come to visit her. "George came in and was absolutely distraught about what had happened. I felt sorry for him."

"He had no clue what Desiree was up to?"

"He said he didn't, and I believe him. Nola came in to visit me, too. She's hoping that now that my attacker is in jail, the police will focus on solving Mama's murder."

"We all want that," Dominique replied. By then they had reached the swamp's entrance. Dominique parked and they both headed in.

"Thanks for coming to get me," Angelique said when they reached Dominique's shanty.

"No problem, and you'll call me if you need anything?" Dominique asked.

"I will, but I'm sure I'll be fine." The two parted ways and Angelique continued on to her shanty.

When she reached it, she went inside and looked around. There was no sign of the life-or-death battle that had occurred in here. She sank down on the sofa.

She had consciously not thought about Daniel the whole time she'd been in the hospital, but now her thoughts were filled with him.

The last time he'd been here, he had saved her life. Had he not come in the front door when he had, there was no doubt in her mind that she would have been killed.

She frowned. And why had he shown up on that night? They hadn't set up a check-in for that night. There had been no reason for his impromptu visit. So, why had he come? And why had it taken her so long to ask him?

It was a question she intended to ask him the next time she saw him. At thoughts of seeing him again, her heart squeezed tight.

She was in love with him. She hadn't wanted to be, she had absolutely fought against it but it had happened. She had fallen deeply in love with him, but her love for him scared her to death.

She got up and went outside and turned on her generator. She needed to make several orders today of items for the store. Then, a week before opening she would go out into the swamp and gather the flowers and foliage she needed to make the all-natural poultices and tinctures she wanted to offer to her patrons.

It was an exciting time for her…the realization of a long-held dream. Hopefully it would fill up the empty hours of the evenings when she'd become so accustomed to sharing time with Daniel.

As if summoned by her thoughts alone, a knock fell on her door and it was the very man she had been thinking about.

"Daniel," she greeted him and her heart expanded with warmth. As usual, he looked ridiculously handsome in his official blue uniform.

"Hi, Angelique." He greeted her with a wide smile that only increased the warmth inside her. "The doctor told me you'd been released today, so I thought I'd come by to see you."

"Come on in." She held the door open wider so he could enter. His familiar scent wrapped around her as he sank down on the sofa. "Would you like something to drink?"

"No, I'm fine. How are you feeling?" His gaze held hers and she wanted to fall into the beautiful blue depths of his eyes.

She sat next to him. "I feel okay…maybe just a little bit tired and my wounds still hurt, but that's to be expected. I was just getting ready to order some things I intend to sell in the store."

"That must be exciting for you."

"It is," she replied. "I'm hoping to have the grand opening in about two weeks."

"Wow, that's a real fast track. Make sure you don't overdo things." There was a deep caring in his gaze.

"I won't."

"You do realize I'm going to continue to do everything in my power to find your mother's killer," he said.

"I know that, but Daniel, I do have a question for you. I was thinking about the night of the attack and I wondered why you showed up here that night? We hadn't made any plans to meet."

"True, we hadn't made plans, but I needed to talk to you that night."

She looked at him in confusion. "Talk to me about what?"

"About how much I love you." His words hung in the air for a long moment, and then he reached for her hand. "Angelique, I'm deeply in love with you. I want to marry you. I want you to have my children and I want to build a future with you."

"Daniel… I…" She started to pull her hand from his, but he held on tight.

"Look me in the eyes, Angelique. Look me in the eyes and tell me you don't love me."

She held his gaze for a long moment and then looked away. She couldn't do it. She couldn't deny her love for him any longer. "Daniel, I am in love with you." The words fell from her on a soft whisper. "But you know how I feel about these things. I don't trust in love."

"Dammit, Angelique, then trust in me." He dropped her hand and instead stood and began to pace in front of her. "There is nothing for you to be afraid of with me. I will love and honor you for as long as we both live, and then I'll continue loving you through eternity."

He paced in front of her as he continued. "Fear is facing a killer who is holding a knife over your chest. Fear is not knowing when an attacker might strike again. But there's no place for fear in love…not in the love I offer to you."

He stopped pacing and fell to a knee in front of her. His eyes shimmered with a wealth of emotion that stole her breath away.

"If you love me, then believe in me," he said softly. "If you really love me, then let your fears go. Make me the happiest man on earth…marry me, Angelique."

"Okay," she replied.

He stared at her for a long moment. "For real?"

She laughed as a rush of sheer happiness winged through her. "Yes, for real."

He grabbed her hands and pulled her up and into his arms. "What made you change your mind?" he asked.

"I lived with fear the whole time Desiree was after me, and when you saved me that night it was like I was gifted a whole new life. I don't want to live in fear anymore. I want to live with you and be your wife. I want to have your babies and…"

His mouth took hers in a kiss that spoke of desire and an everlasting love. When the kiss ended, he held her gaze. "Do you promise to keep me safe from dancing deer in pink bikinis?"

She laughed. "I promise," she replied. "You are such a goof."

"I'm your goof," he replied and then claimed her

lips once again. She kissed him with all the love she had in her heart. She trusted in him. More than anything she trusted in them. Together they were going to have a marvelous life together, and she couldn't wait for it to begin.

* * * * *